"I hope it is not too dull for you?"

"Dull?" Charity was astonished at his question. "How could it possibly be dull? I've loved every minute of it."

They walked halfway across the hospital entrance before she stopped. Tyco van der Brons stood looking down at her, not smiling. "Tell me, do you like me?"

She smiled widely at him. "Oh, yes, indeed, I do. You're—you're safe, if you know what I mean."

His expression didn't alter. "You mean that I'm not like van Kamp, that I'm not likely to play havoc with your heart," he said evenly. "Does he still do that?"

She thought for a moment. "Well, just now and then. But I've learned my lesson."

Betty Neels is well-known for her romances set in the Netherlands, which is hardly surprising. She married a Dutchman and spent the first twelve years of their marriage living in Holland and working as a nurse. Today, she and her husband make their home in a small, ancient stone cottage in England's West Country, but they return to Holland often. She loves to explore tiny villages and tour privately owned homes there in order to lend an air of authenticity to the background of her books.

THE FINAL TOUCH
Betty Neels

Harlequin Books

TORONTO • NEW YORK • LONDON
AMSTERDAM • PARIS • SYDNEY • HAMBURG
STOCKHOLM • ATHENS • TOKYO • MILAN
MADRID • WARSAW • BUDAPEST • AUCKLAND

To Maartje and Henry

Original hardcover edition published in 1991
by Mills & Boon Limited

ISBN 0-373-03197-1

Harlequin Romance first edition May 1992

THE FINAL TOUCH

CHAPTER ONE

THE vast entrance hall of one of Amsterdam's oldest and largest hospitals was very nearly empty. At eight o'clock in the evening, visitors had gone home and the chilly dark of a November evening had kept those of the hospital staff who were free indoors. There were, however, four people there: the porter in his kiosk, a telephonist manning a switchboard tucked away at the back of the hall and two men standing near the entrance, deep in talk—an elderly man with white hair and a flowing moustache and beard, not much above middle height and pretty portly, and his companion, strongly built and towering above him, his handsome head bent as he listened, the dim light above them turning his grizzled head to dull silver. The older man spoke at some length, pausing only when someone came in through the big swing doors. A girl, neatly dressed in a raincoat which had seen better days, a headscarf and sensible shoes. She took off the scarf as she crossed the hall, uncovering light brown hair pinned into a bun, and then ducked her head into the kiosk.

The two men watched her and the elder said softly, 'The English nurse—you have not yet met her? She is good: capable and quick and does not fuss. She has no Dutch to speak of but she is learning fast.' He added thoughtfully, 'A rather plain girl and I think not happy.'

'Homesick?' The question was casually kind.

'No, no. I believe she has no home. Young van Kamp met her when he was doing that course in London, took her here, there and everywhere and persuaded her to try for a job with us. Well, we all know van Kamp, don't we? A great one for the girls, and that's all right as long as they don't take him seriously. Only it seems that she has taken him seriously. He has taken her out once or twice but I hear that he has his eye on that new young woman on Men's Medical.'

They watched the girl leave the kiosk and disappear down one of the corridors leading from the hall.

'You are very well informed,' remarked the younger man.

'Huib——' Huib was his registrar '—hears all this from the junior housemen. He thinks it is a great shame; he wants to warn her, but, although she is well liked, there is no one close enough.' He shrugged his shoulders. 'But there, she is a young woman of twenty-three and presumably doesn't walk around with her head in a sack. Now, as to this patient...'

The girl, in the meanwhile, had made her way to the nurses' home and gone to her room. Her head was by no means in a sack but for some months it had been in the clouds, kept there by daydreams of a happy future, but now, sitting on the side of her bed, still in her raincoat, she had to admit that the sooner she got her feet back on solid earth, the better. She had been a fool, but never again, she told herself fiercely. Sitting there, she went over the events of the last month or so and, being a girl of good sense, admitted that she had been blind and naïve; Cor van Kamp had swept her off her feet just at a time when she had been fighting discontent with her life. She was happy as a nurse and she had done well but her home-life was non-existent. Her mother had died when she was still at school and her father had remarried after a few years; a widow with a daughter a little older than she—company for each other, her father had declared happily, only it hadn't worked out like that. Her stepsister Eunice had grown into a pretty girl, found herself a job as a fashion model and left home, and shortly after that her father had died and her stepmother had sold their home and gone to live in the South of France. Within a year she had lost all contact with her and she saw Eunice only in the pages of glossy magazines. The tentative advances she had made to meet, even to find a small flat and share it, had been rebuffed.

She had known at the time that it had been silly to suggest it; she had almost nothing in common with her stepsister and she was aware that her ordinary features, old-fashioned ideas and lack of clever conversation would have been a hindrance to Eunice. Besides, she wore all the wrong clothes... Cor van Kamp had changed all that for her; he had singled her out, talked to her, taken her to romantic little restaurants for dinner, walked with her in the parks of London, borrowed a car and taken her to Brighton for the day, to the theatre, to films... She had been infatuated, believing every word he told her—that she was the only girl for him and hinting at a marvellous future—unaware that he had been amusing himself. He had not wanted to go to London in the first place and he was bored, and then he had seen her and set himself the task of getting her to fall in love with him just for a joke. He had suggested that she might get a job at his own hospital in Amsterdam even though he hadn't

meant a word of it; indeed, he was getting bored with
her too. She was a nice little thing, but he was clever
enough to realise that she was a girl with decided ideas
about brief love-affairs, and she was tiresomely serious
about marriage. All the same, he had found it all a
bit of a joke when she had left her job at the hospital
and applied for and got the post of staff nurse on
Women's Surgical in Amsterdam.

That had been almost two months ago and during
that time they had been out together only three times,
brief meetings in cafés when he had talked easily and
amusingly about the hospital and his work and never
about their future together. He had kissed her carelessly and told her how much he missed her but that
he had almost no free time. She had believed him,
holding desperately on to the excuse that he worked
even harder than she did, and on their last meeting
she had tried hard not to notice that he was preoccupied, even impatient with her. All the same, she had
told him that she would have a half-day at the weekend
and could they meet, and everything had been all right
again when he had said at once that there was nothing
he'd rather do than be with her and told her to wait
for him in the Rijksmuseum. 'Sit in front of the
Nachtwacht,' he had told her. 'I may get held up, but
I'll come.'

It had rained, but she hadn't minded that. She had
hurried off duty, eaten a hasty lunch and changed out
of her uniform, boarded a tram and filed into the
museum with a sprinkling of tourists and locals
anxious to get out of the chilly November rain. The
row of chairs before the famous painting was empty;
she chose a seat in the centre and composed herself

to wait. From time to time someone would come and sit down near her, the better to study the magnificent painting, but time wore on and Cor didn't come. However, he had said wait, so she waited while the afternoon edged itself into dusk and one of the attendants came to tell her that the museum would be closing very shortly.

So she went back into the damp streets, uncertain what to do. She had no idea where he might be. The best thing to do would be to go back to the hospital and ask at the porter's lodge; Cor might have left a message... The thought cheered her and she went into a coffee shop and had coffee and a spiced bun before getting on a tram once more. The tram was full of people in damp coats and she had to stand, her small slender person jammed between two stout matrons with laden shopping bags. The tram stopped close to the hospital but on the other side of the busy street and she had to wait for a gap in the traffic. Visitors were streaming out of the hospital forecourt and she glanced at her watch. It was just after half-past six, and if Cor was free there was still time for them to go out to dinner or to a film.

He was free—she saw him a moment later—but not for her. He had strolled on to the opposite pavement, his arm tucked into that of a girl—one of the staff nurses in Theatre whom she knew slightly. As she looked he bent his head and kissed her and they laughed together and went walking off, still laughing.

She watched them go and all the small doubts she had tried so hard to ignore during the last few weeks came crowding back, presenting her with a clear picture quite unlike her dreams. She turned on her heel and walked back towards the shopping streets, their windows still lighted, and went from shop to shop, gazing unseeingly at their displays, but it kept her from thinking. It was striking eight o'clock when she went through the doors into the entrance hall and asked in her quiet voice if there had been a message for her, knowing already that there hadn't.

Now she sat on her bed, doing her best to think sensibly. She couldn't pack her bags and go; she had a contract for six months and, besides, she had nowhere to go, and she had to see Cor; there might be some good reason...

She got up and studied her face in the looking-glass. It looked exactly the same as usual, a little pale perhaps, but her nice unremarkable face showed no sign of her troubled thoughts. She tidied her hair, used powder and lipstick, and went down to the canteen for her supper.

When her companions asked her if she had had a pleasant half-day, she replied serenely that she had enjoyed herself immensely. Only Zuster Smit, another of the staff nurses in Theatre, gave her a faintly surprised and thoughtful look; she went out occasionally with one of the house surgeons and had been told something of the reason why the English girl had come to the hospital. Charity Pearson was a nice girl and deserved better; besides, she was in a strange country. Zuster Smit finished her supper, wondering uneasily if she should do something about it. Warn Charity that van Kamp wasn't serious and seemed unlikely to be in the foreseeable future? Mention casually that he was free for two or three evenings each week? And that he dated a different nurse each time?

She found herself unable to do any of these things. She could mention it to the houseman she was friendly with, and ask him to talk to van Kamp. That wouldn't do either. She leaned across the table and invited Charity to have a mug of coffee in her room with half a dozen other nurses; she hadn't eaten her supper and she was pale and quieter than ever.

It was Theatre day on Women's Surgical the next morning, something Charity welcomed for she was kept too busy to think about anything but her work. The routine was familiar by now and very similar to that of the London hospital where she had trained, and she had acquired a basic Dutch so that she could answer the patients' needs; she went to and fro with the cases for Theatre, saw to drips, inspected dressings and, under the *Hoofdzuster*'s sharp eye, gave necessary injections. She was off duty at five o'clock but it was nearer six by the time she left the ward and began the lengthy walk through the hospital to the nurses' home. The surgical wing was new, built on to the original main hospital, and the women's ward was on the third floor. She went slowly down the wide staircase to the floor below—the floor where Cor worked, although on the other side of the main building, where the medical wards were housed. Tired though she was, she allowed her feet to carry her along the wide corridor at the back of the old hospital— there was just the chance that she might meet Cor. She had never gone to that wing deliberately before but now it seemed to her urgent to see him. She was halfway along it when he came out of the swing doors of the children's ward, saw her, hesitated, and then came towards her.

'Darling...' he was smiling at her '...I've been trying to see you all day—but I'm up to my eyes and still hard at it. I'm so sorry about yesterday—an emergency—didn't have time to leave a message for you; actually I was in Theatre until after midnight, giving anaesthetics.'

Charity looked at him without smiling, willing him to tell the truth and beg her to forgive him, but he stood there, smiling still.

After a silence which went on far too long she said in her quiet voice, 'No, you weren't, Cor. I saw you yesterday evening with that pretty staff nurse from Theatre. You were on the pavement outside the hospital.' She went on steadily, 'Oh, it's quite all right—it's me that's been silly—I thought... Well, never mind what I thought, but you didn't need to lie.'

He blustered a bit then. 'I don't know what you mean—there's no harm in a man's taking a girl out.'

'None at all, only you weren't very fair, were you? I sat in the Rijksmuseum for hours. Did you forget?'

'No, no, of course not; I thought you'd have the sense not to wait for more than half an hour or so.' He smiled again—he smiled too easily, she thought. 'Anyway, no harm done. We had fun together while it lasted, darling, and you've got a good job here.'

'Yes, I have.' Her voice was suddenly sharp. 'And don't ever call me darling again.'

His smile became a sneer. 'Oh, be your age, for heaven's sake—good lord, you would think I had intended marrying you.'

When she stayed silent he said, 'My God, you did... You must have been out of your mind.'

She said, her voice quite quiet once more, 'Yes, I think I was, but I'm sane now.' And, suddenly impatient, she added, 'Oh, go away, do.'

He turned on his heel and went without a backward glance, leaving her standing there, watched with calm interest by the man who had come from the children's ward. Only when he saw her take out a handkerchief and blow her small nose with unwonted vigour did he put out a hand behind him, push the door soundlessly open and then allow it to swing back with some force so that she was aware of someone there. She didn't turn round. He hadn't expected her to; he walked past her rigid back without haste on his way to the medical wing and he was very nearly at the end of the corridor when he heard her muffled sobs.

He walked back to where she was standing. 'Staff Nurse Pearson, is it not?' He had only the faintest of accents and his voice was quiet. 'Perhaps I can help?'

She hadn't turned round and her sniffs were prodigious but she answered him at once. 'Thank you— but not really, please don't bother.'

He said easily, 'You haven't been here long, have you? I expect you are feeling homesick, are you not? I was just going out for a breath of air and a cup of coffee. Why not come with me? And do turn round; there is nothing to be ashamed of in tears, you know.'

He had a compelling voice, she turned round obediently and lifted her face, rendered plain by tears and a pink nose, to his. She hadn't seen him before; she was sure that she would have remembered him if she had. He was quite overpoweringly tall and massively built and good-looking into the bargain. 'Are you a visitor?' she asked.

'Er—no, I work here.'

'A doctor?'

'A surgeon.' He smiled down at her very kindly. 'Van der Brons.' He put out a large firm hand and engulfed one of hers. 'Go and put on a coat; I'll be in the entrance hall in ten minutes.'

He saw her hesitate and added gently, 'And wear something on your head—it's a chilly evening.'

His prosaic remark was somehow reassuring.

He was in the entrance hall when she got there ten minutes later, looking larger than ever in a thick jacket, his silvery head uncovered. The jacket looked expensive and she wondered uneasily just who he was but his friendly, 'Ah, there you are,' dispelled any vague doubts and they went out into the courtyard together and thence into the busy street. It was a chilly damp evening and the streets around the hospital were narrow with ancient houses brooding over them. He took her arm and led her through the narrow alley which brought them out into a better-lit street.

'Coffee first?' he asked, and didn't wait for an answer but steered her into a half-empty café and sat her down at a small table. It was very warm there, and he took her raincoat and tossed his jacket over the back of his chair, revealing a beautifully tailored suit, immaculate linen and gold cufflinks. Her uneasy thoughts returned but were swept away by his easy, 'Toasted sandwiches? And *uitsmijter*? Soup?'

She chose sandwiches, he gave the order and they drank their coffee while they waited. However upset she felt, she was given no chance to brood, for he kept up a steady flow of small talk about nothing in particular.

The sandwiches were delicious and the coffee hot and comforting; Charity's pale face resumed its normal healthy colour and, led on in a gentle way by her companion, she began to talk, not noticing that his casual questions were encouraging her to tell him something of herself.

He fetched more coffee from the crowded counter and asked carelessly, 'Do you intend to stay in Holland for a time or is this just a few months' visit to see if you like us?'

She didn't answer at once. She had a sudden wish to spill her bewilderment and misery and loneliness all over this large placid man, but of course that was an idiotic idea; she didn't even know who he was, only his name and the fact that he was a surgeon at the hospital. She blushed scarlet, remembering that she and Cor had met in a similar fashion. Perhaps this man had picked her up on the spur of the moment, and how willingly she had agreed to go with him!

Mr van der Brons, watching her, guessed unerringly what was in her head. 'I have a sister about your age,' he said in a soothing voice. 'She's in Edinburgh on a six-month course; she qualified here, now she wants to spread her wings—just as you. She is the youngest—I have two other sisters and two brothers. Have you any brothers and sisters?'

Somehow he had conveyed the impression that he was her elder brother too, so she said readily, 'No, at least—I have a stepsister. She's a model and lives in London. She's very pretty...'

'Your parents?' The question was so softly put that she hardly noticed it.

'My mother died when I was still a small girl, and my father married again—my stepmother was a widow and had a little girl too. He died just after I started my training and my stepmother has gone to live in the South of France.'

Before she could regret her chattiness he began to talk about his own family, vague remarks which in truth told her nothing about him or them but allayed her shyness and doubts.

'Do you care for a brisk walk? It will have to be up one street and down another but some of the buildings are charming and the canals are always interesting.' He glanced at his watch. 'Are you on duty in the morning?' And when she nodded, 'Then we have time to walk for half an hour before you need to be back.'

They went out into the dark evening and he took her arm to cross the street. 'Do you find the duty hours easier here?'

'Well, seven o'clock is earlier then I was used to in London.' She had to skip a bit to keep up with him and he slowed his steps. 'On the other hand, it is nice to be off duty earlier; I mean, half-past three is very handy if one wants to go shopping.'

He agreed gravely as they started to walk alongside a canal, along a cobbled street lined with gabled houses, their windows lighted, the curtains undrawn. He pointed out the variety of gables to her, described their interiors, remarking that for the most part their owners took great pride in keeping them in good order.

'They look delightful from outside,' said Charity, 'I hope I get the chance to see inside one before I go back to England.'

'Well, there's time enough for that, is there not? Do you have a six-month contract?'

'Yes.' His remark reminded her of her talk with Cor and a very sharp wave of unhappiness washed over her so that she was quite unable to say anything more; just for a little while this nice quiet man had pushed away a future she didn't want to think about but now it was back again. She drew a troubled breath and made a great point of examining the contents of a small antiques shop they were passing, doing her best to regain her usual good sense.

'You're unhappy,' he stated in a matter-of-fact voice, 'and I find it difficult to believe that you are homesick since you have no home, but I dare say you don't want to talk about it, not just now.'

He turned her round and began to walk back the way they had come. When they were within sight of the hospital she asked, 'Why did you ask me to come out with you?'

'I told you that I have a sister about your age; I would like to think that if she were unhappy and alone in Edinburgh there would be someone to keep her company for an hour or two, since I couldn't do that myself.'

'Oh—oh, I see. Well, thank you very much—you've been very kind. I feel quite all right again. I'm not usually so silly...'

He pushed open the big door and held it for her to go through. 'There is nothing silly about admitting one's feelings.' He smiled very kindly at her upturned face. 'Now go to bed and sleep well.'

'You too, Mr van der Brons.'

He waited near the door until she had disappeared from the hall and then turned and went out again to where a dark grey Rolls-Royce was parked, got in and drove away.

Charity hadn't expected to sleep, but she did, only to wake very early to face a day she would have to get through somehow. She supposed that in a little while she would feel happy again but on this dark cold morning the future seemed a hopeless blank. In vain she told herself that Cor wasn't worth another

thought, that she was well out of it. She would forget
him in time, and when her contract was up she would
go back to England and get a good post in one of the
teaching hospitals and carve a career for herself. The
thought depressed her but at least it was something
to think about.

She joined her fellow nurses at breakfast, out-
wardly her usual quiet self, answering their good-
natured remarks in her peculiar Dutch and then hurrying through the hospital to her ward.

Ladies who had been operated on the previous day
were feeling, naturally enough, low-spirited and the
Hoofdzuster, a rather peevish woman at the best of
times, had started a cold so that her peevishness was
even worse than usual. Charity, doing her best, was
glad that she was off duty at half-past three. If she
were quick, there would be time to go to the book
shop on the Singel and choose a paperback. Books
were expensive in Holland, she had discovered, but
they were her only extravagance.

When her father had died the allowance he had
given her had been stopped by her stepmother, who
had pointed out that now that she was nursing she
earned enough to be independent. She had added, 'I
know that in his will your father arranged for me to
continue your allowance but of course when he went
to make it you were still at school. I don't believe in
young people living on money they haven't earned.
You are not like Eunice, who will probably marry well;
you need to work hard and make a career for yourself.'
She had left for France shortly after that, taking every
penny with her.

There was nothing to be done about that; Charity,
never an extravagant girl, learned to buy the sort of

clothes which didn't date and made them last and, since although she was well liked at the hospital she was seldom asked out, that didn't matter too much. If sometimes she envied her friends' new outfits and sighed over the glamorous photos of Eunice in the glossy magazines she never mentioned it.

Now, hurrying towards the shops in the Kalverstraat and Leidsestraat, she decided that the time had come to buy something new and for once fashionable. She had saved for a rainy day and this seemed to be it. She chose a book and then turned her attention to the dress shops. They were all too expensive; C & A and Vroom and Dressman would suit her pocket better. It was a pity that there wasn't time to buy anything before they closed but she studied their windows so that on her next free day she would have some idea of what she wanted. Her winter coat was good for another year; it had been bought in a sale, a serviceable brown wool bearing a quality label. She had a couple of skirts too and jumpers and sweaters enough even if she was heartily sick of them. A really smart dress, she mused, some pretty shoes and, if there was enough money, a pair of soft leather boots. She walked back to the hospital, keeping her mind on new clothes and off Cor, who most tiresomely lurked at the back of her head however she tried to forget him; it was a pity that she should walk into him as she reached the hospital forecourt. He stopped in front of her and started to speak, but she brushed past him, her chin in the air, and Mr van der Brons, standing at the ward window high above her, nodded his head in approval.

Charity plunged wholeheartedly into her work; it wasn't too bad on the ward for her head was occupied

with the different jobs she was doing and struggling
to speak a coherent Dutch which the patients could
understand. They were all very good to her, making
her repeat a new word until she had it right so that
she began to achieve quite a vocabulary, albeit with
a marked Amsterdam accent. She got on well with
the other nurses too and once or twice went out to
the cinema with them or to a café for a cheap meal,
but even so there were still times when she was alone
and unable to do anything but think of Cor. It should
have helped her to forget him when snippets of gossip
reached her ears, dropped by kindly nurses who had
put two and two together about her and Cor and considered that he had treated her badly, but none of the
tales of the light-hearted affairs with first one nurse
and then another had eased her feelings. It was the
first time she had fallen in love so wholeheartedly and
she was incapable of knowing the difference between
that and infatuation. However, she was sensible
enough to know that she couldn't sit around and
mope. She began to make a systematic round of the
city's museums and botanical gardens; quite a few of
them were free and in others the charges were small.
She tried Madame Tussaud's wax models of the Dutch
through the ages and balanced that visit, which was
expensive, by spending half a day at the Museum
Architectuur, which was free, and of course she went
again to the Rijksmuseum, for as well as the paintings
there, the displays of silver and glass and furniture
were enormous; it would probably take her until the
end of her stay to see it all.

Once or twice she thought about Mr van der Brons;
she had never seen him again and she began to wonder
if he had been a visitor, enjoying a joke at her ex-

pense, but even if that were the case she thought of him with pleasure and a little wistfully, for he had proved a friend in need without offering tiresome advice or being too sympathetic.

It would have surprised her to know that he was aware of her comings and goings.

He was in Brussels when she was moved to Men's Medical, which meant that she saw Cor each and every day, not always to speak to, of course, but, all the same, even if he were at the other end of the ward, she was unhappily aware of him and it took all her self-control to attend him while he examined a patient. As for Cor, he found the situation amusing and took every opportunity to speak to her, putting a hand on her shoulder for good measure as he passed her, giving her speaking glances, exchanging knowing looks with the patients. She had to put up with it, for she had no reason other than to get away from him with which to plead to the *directrice* to have her moved to another ward. The *Hoofdzuster* had given her a good report after her first week and she enjoyed her work there. It seemed as though she would have to bear with his unwelcome attentions. For they were unwelcome, despite the fact that she still thought of him with longing, for every time he came on to the ward—and that was often enough—the sight of him set her heart beating and brought the pretty colour into her cheeks. Just the same she began to look plain and pale; there were shadows under her eyes and her slim person became thin.

This was something which Mr van der Brons noticed at once when he came on to the ward to give his opinion on a patient needing plastic surgery. He was accompanied by his registrar, a posse of housemen and the medical consultant of the ward, and met at the door by the *Hoofdzuster* with suitable pomp. Charity, busy getting old Mijnheer Prins back into his bed, looked up as the party proceeded down the ward, her firm little chin dropping with utter surprise, remembering just in time to uphold the tottering Mijnheer Prins before his old legs gave out, while a nice warm feeling crept around her insides. Rather like seeing a comfy chair by a bright fire on a cold day, she thought confusedly, or finding the right path when you thought you were lost.

Mr van der Brons came unhurriedly down the ward, his head bent to catch whatever it was his colleague was saying, but he glanced up and smiled very faintly at her as the entourage swept past. She didn't smile back at him; it might not do. She beamed at her patient instead as she heaved him carefully between the sheets.

Mr van der Brons, back in his consulting-room on the ground floor of the hospital, made no effort to do any work but sat deep in thought until it was time for him to go to his own operating theatre and deal with a particularly nasty case of burns needing skin grafts. Scrubbing presently with his registrar at the next basin, he remarked casually, 'I saw that man on Medical this morning; we had better fit him in next week. He's well enough, I think. I see the English nurse is working there...'

'Yes—van Kamp was talking about that the other day, so one of the housemen told me. Everyone knows how shabbily he has behaved and it is a shame; she's a nice girl too and has never uttered a word against him. More than he deserves. He should keep to his own sort. I'm told he needles her when he's on the ward.'

Mr van der Brons, standing obediently while a nurse fastened his gown about his vast frame, merely grunted.

Two days later, Charity was told that she had been posted to the burns unit. 'You're a lucky girl,' observed the *Hoofdzuster*, who was sorry to see her go. 'Mr van der Brons is highly thought of. The burns unit is quite a large one and always very busy. I hope you will be happy there, Zuster Pearson.'

Charity had absolutely no doubt about that; she was free of Cor and with a chance of forgetting him and working for a man she had instantly liked.

CHAPTER TWO

THE burns unit was modern, built on to the original hospital, equipped with the most up-to-date beds, operating theatres and recovery-rooms. It could house twenty patients and was always full for hospitals from the surrounding countryside sent their patients there to be treated and, later, to have skin grafts. Charity, presenting herself for duty on a Monday morning, marvelled at the wealth of apparatus as she found her way to Sister's office. Hoofdzuster Kingsma was sitting at her desk, a splendid figure of a young woman with regular features, very blue eyes and pale hair. She looked up as Charity tapped on the door and went in and said pleasantly in heavily accented English, 'Ah, the new member of our team. It is nice to meet you, Zuster Pearson. Sit, please, and I will tell you of our unit and your duties and then we will go together and see all of it.'

So Charity sat and listened carefully; she wouldn't be able to remember it all at once but she stored the information away, especially the last bit of her companion's briefing. 'You will expect, you understand, to work hard,' she observed cheerfully. 'The professor will have only the best; he does not look at the clock and he would not expect any of us to do so either. If we are off duty and he is still working, then we stay on duty. You understand? He is a hard taskmaster but he is also a very good man and most kind.'

Charity nodded her tidy head under its little white cap. She wondered who the professor might be. Perhaps Mr van der Brons was his registrar. She would have to find out...

She found out within seconds of the thought. Mr van der Brons came into the office and Zuster Kingsma rustled to her feet and said, '*Goeden morgen*, Professor.' Charity, on her feet as well, murmured, 'Good morning,' with suitable politeness.

Quite wasted on him, for he clapped Hoofdzuster Kingsma on the shoulder with a friendly, '*Dag, Els*,' and asked Charity if she was pleased to be working on the burns unit. 'Hard, very hard work, Charity,' he added 'but I dare say you will enjoy it.'

'I am just about to take Zuster Pearson round the department,' said Hoofdzuster Kingsma, 'but perhaps you wish to see a patient?'

The pair of them switched to speaking in Dutch then, which gave Charity time to look at him properly, something she had never quite achieved. She had, she remembered been too upset about Cor...

He was older than she had first thought, nearer forty than thirty, and undeniably good-looking... He turned his head suddenly and gave her a kind smile; his eyes were very blue, even more so than *Hoofdzuster*'s, half hidden under heavy lids. He said in English, 'Sister will report on you in a week's time. If you are not happy with us, don't be afraid to say so, but I see no reason why you shouldn't settle in nicely.'

He nodded in an absent-minded way and went off, leaving Hoofdzuster Kingsma to guide her round the department. It took quite a time, what with being introduced to the other nurses—and there was no lack of staff—and meeting the patients. There was a small ward for children, all four cots occupied; three of them had been scalded. 'Hot coffee,' explained Sister, 'boiling water from the cooking-stove, and this one climbed into a bath—her mother had filled it with scalding water and gone to answer the telephone—and this one...' she paused by a little boy of seven or eight years '...is to have a skin graft. He was here for four months last year; now the professor is going to repair the damage. His back is a mass of scar tissue—he will need several grafts over the next few years.'

She led the way to a large airy room where four women sat in comfortable chairs, knitting and sewing. 'All for grafts,' said Sister. 'Do you know anything about grafting?'

'Not very much, Sister. There's the Thiersch method, isn't there? Small pieces of skin bound on to the raw area? And Reverdin's method—I've not seen that one—strips of skin taken from an arm or a thigh...'

'That is right, we see both those here, and also the professor works a great deal with pedicles—he has had some splendid results.'

There was a men's ward with six beds and another ward with women patients and two six-wards, both occupied. There was a splendidly equipped intensive care unit too. Charity followed the *Hoofdzuster* back to her office, reflecting that while she was on duty she was unlikely to have a moment in which to allow her thoughts to wander, and when she did get off duty she would probably be too tired to do more than climb into her bed. She found that she welcomed the thought; she would have no chance to mope over Cor and since the burns unit was in a separate wing of the hospital she wasn't likely to meet him either.

She sat down in front of Hoofdzuster Kingsma's desk and paid strict attention to what she was saying. 'Now, as for the patients who come to us with burns, there is much to be done for them, and on admission the professor or his registrar will be present. There is shock and much pain and loss of fluid, of that you will already know—yes? And its treatment? Good. Morphia is given intravenously—the professor himself orders exactly what he wishes done.'

Charity spent the next few days getting to know her way around. She saw little or nothing of Mr van der Brons for the simple reason that she worked only on the wards where patients were either waiting for skin grafts or were being treated for comparatively minor burns. True, he came on to these wards, but most of his day was spent in Theatre or doing the dressings of his most badly injured patients, for these he liked to attend to himself.

It was at the end of her first week, with the prospect of a free day ahead of her, that she came face to face with him on her way off duty. He stood in front of her with the air of a man who had all day at his disposal. 'Ah, going off duty? Do you like your work here?'

'Yes. Oh, yes, very much—it's different...'

'Indeed it is. Have you done any Theatre work?'

'Not very much. Only three months' staffing. I enjoyed it.'

'Then very soon you shall come into Theatre. Are you off duty now?'

'Yes, sir.'

'Good. We will spend the evening together and you shall tell me what you think of the unit.' He glanced at his watch. 'Twenty minutes? I'll be in the forecourt.'

Charity grabbed at common sense as the prospect of an evening spent in his company threatened to swamp it. 'That's very kind of you, sir, but I'm not sure . . .'

'Why not? I don't bite. There is no time to discuss things while we are both working. We can do so at our leisure.'

Put like that it sounded completely sensible; moreover, she could think of no reasonable excuse.

She said in her quiet way, 'Well, thank you. I'll— I'll go and change.'

She went past him and then stopped. 'Nowhere too grand,' she begged him. 'I haven't the right clothes.'

He assured her in a placid manner that the restaurant he had in mind required no dressing up.

She showered and changed into a soft grey jersey dress which, while well cut and in the best of taste, did nothing for her, topped it with her winter coat, dug her feet into her best shoes—quite unsuitable for the Dutch winter weather—found gloves and handbag, and went down to the entrance, telling herself as she went that she must have lost her good sense. Mr van der Brons could have found out all he wanted to know about her reactions to working at the hospital without the bother of taking her out for the evening. She made her way to the entrance, worrying as to whether she was wearing the right clothes. Cor had never happened to take her anywhere where clothes mattered, but she had the strong feeling that the professor was an entirely different kettle of fish.

She had worried unnecessarily; she was stuffed neatly into the Rolls and driven through the city to the Bodega Keijzer, opposite the Concertgebow, for the professor had a very shrewd idea of what she was thinking about behind her quiet face. The food there was excellent and the atmosphere was pleasantly warm and friendly, just the thing to put her at her ease, and the grey dress was exactly right... Charity relaxed, which was what he had intended, drank the sherry he ordered for her and conned the menu.

'I'm famished,' observed Mr van der Brons. 'The *groentensoup* is delicious; shall we have that to start with? And the fish here is good—I can recommend the *zeetong*—sole...'

Charity, disarmed by the friendly informal atmosphere, agreed happily and applied herself to her soup and the easygoing conversation of her companion. They had eaten their soup and sole and she was halfway through a towering ice-cream swathed in whipped cream before Mr van der Brons asked her if she was happy.

She paused in conveying a spoonful of ice to her mouth. 'Me? Yes, thank you. I do like the burns unit; it's—it's worthwhile, if you see what I mean.'

The professor, whose life work it was, saw what she meant. 'Not working you too hard?' he wanted to know pleasantly.

'No. It's nice to be so busy that there's no time to think about anything else.'

She blushed a little, for she hadn't meant to say that; it was a relief when he took no notice. He would have forgotten about Cor by now.

She swallowed the next spoonful of ice-cream very suddenly when he asked. 'And young van Kamp?'

He expected an answer, she could see that. 'I never see him,' she told him, but she couldn't quite keep the regret out of her voice.

He said kindly, 'You have only to ask me if you should at any time wish to be transferred back to a medical ward.'

She said hastily, 'No, that would be a mistake—he might think that I was... He's taking out that very pretty nurse from the general theatre.'

'Ah, yes. She is a charmer, isn't she? Will you have another ice? No? Coffee, then... Do you hear from your stepsister?'

'I had a card from Portugal, she's modelling there for *Harper's and Queen* magazine.'

'It is to be hoped that she will get an assignment to Amsterdam, then you would be able to spend some time with her.'

'It would be nice to see her.' She looked down at her plate. 'But I bore her and I can quite see why. She is really beautiful.' She sighed unconsciously. 'And she wears the loveliest clothes.'

She didn't enlarge upon that; somehow she felt that her companion didn't mind about clothes, though without saying a word he had given her the impression that he had found the grey dress quite acceptable.

She gave another little sigh, this time of pure pleasure; Mr van der Brons was an undemanding and restful companion. With Cor she had had to exert herself to be lively and appreciative of his remarks; with her companion there was no need to be either. Indeed, their small talk was easy and their silences were comfortable and there was no need to break them; she was quite at ease with him.

They sat over their meal for a long time until she glanced at her watch and exclaimed at the lateness of the hour.

'You have a day off tomorrow,' he pointed out. When she nodded without speaking, he asked, 'What do you intend to do with it? A week tomorrow I'm going to Leiden...'

He was sitting back in his chair, a cup of coffee before him. 'I am lecturing there. I'll give you a lift there, only you will have to be outside by half-past eight.' He smiled suddenly so that she found herself smiling back, when in actual fact she had intended refusing coldly, for he had sounded arbitrary.

She said hesitantly, 'Well...' Of course he would be used to his sisters; she imagined that an elder brother might adopt a tone of voice like that when addressing them; perhaps he thought of her in the same category. 'Thank you very much,' she said in a little rush.

He took her back to the hospital presently, bade her a pleasant goodnight at the entrance and waited until she had disappeared down the corridor on her way to the nurses' residence before getting back into his car and driving himself home.

He was letting himself into one of the beautiful seventeenth-century red brick town houses overlooking the Herengracht when he was met in his hall by a small neat man of middle years who addressed him with the civil familiarity of an old servant and a decided cockney accent.

'Evening, Jolly,' said the professor.

'Good evening to you, sir—me and Mrs J. were getting that worried. As nice a dinner as I ever seen all ready to serve and you not 'ome.'

He took his master's coat and laid it carefully over an arm. 'Rang the 'ospital, I did, and they said as you 'ad gone hours earlier.' .

'On a friendly impulse I took someone out to dinner, Jolly. I had no intention of doing so, but she looked very lonely. English, Jolly.'

'Ah, a tourist, sir?'

'No, a nurse at the hospital. So I will come to the kitchen and apologise to Mrs Jolly and beg you to eat the dinner she had so kindly cooked for me.'

'Well, as to that, sir...' Jolly bustled ahead and opened the narrow door at the back of the hall and they descended a few steps to the kitchen, an extremely cosy place even if semi-basement; warm and well lit with a vast Aga along one wall and an open dresser filled with china along another. There were Windsor chairs on either side of the Aga, each occupied by a cat, and sprawled before the fire was a large shaggy dog who heaved himself up and pranced to meet the professor. He stayed quietly by him while he made his excuses to his housekeeper, speaking Dutch this time to the plump little woman before going back to the hall and into his study, the dog close on his heels. Here he sat down at his desk and, despite the papers waiting for his attention, did nothing at all for quite a while but sat deep in thought.

Presently he stirred. 'I am almost forty years old,' he addressed the dog, who looked intelligent and wagged his tail. 'Would you consider, Samson, that I am middle-aged? Past the first flush of youth? Becoming set in my ways?'

Samson rumbled gently in a negative fashion and the professor said, 'Oh, good, I value your opinion, Samson.' He pulled the papers towards him and applied himself to them. 'She has a day off tomorrow,' he went on, 'but I shall see her after that . . .'

He saw her the next day under rather trying circumstances.

Charity had gone out early; it was a cold clear day, frosty, with a blue sky and a hint of snow to come. Since she wasn't going to Leiden until next week she had her day planned; she intended to follow the Singel Gracht, the outermost *gracht* of the inner city, from one end to the other, and when she had done that she would spend an hour or two in a museum and treat herself to a meal in a coffee shop. She had planned to buy some new clothes but somehow she felt restless and a day spent walking and getting to know Amsterdam suited her mood.

She kept to the Singel for some time and then just past the Leidse Plein she crossed over to the Lijnbaans Gracht; she was approaching the Jordaan now, its streets named after flowers and plants, for Jordaan was a corruption of Jardin. Presently she wandered down one of them to become happily lost in a maze of narrow streets lined with small old houses, threaded with narrow canals. She was almost at the end of one such street when she saw smoke billowing from the upper window of a gabled house, bent with age, seemingly held upright by its neighbours. There was no one about, since it was that time in the morning when even the most hardworking of housewives stopped for her cup of coffee. Charity raced down the street and banged on the house door, yelling, 'Fire,' at the top of her voice. No one appeared to hear, understandably, for somewhere close by there was a radio blaring pop music.

No one came to the door; she thumped again, still shouting, and then tried the handle. The door opened and she plunged inside. The smoke was rolling down the narrow ladder-like staircase leading from the tiny hall but there were no flames yet. She looked into the room downstairs, cast an urgent eye into the tiny kitchen behind it, tore a towel from a hook on the wall, splashed water over it, and, holding it to her face, began to climb the stairs.

They led to one room under the roof, with a small window at each end, furnished with a large bed, a chest of drawers, a chair or two and a cot under the back window, all of them shrouded in thick smoke. There was a baby in the cot and, lying by an over-turned oil stove, there was a toddler, clothes alight, screaming in terror and pain. Charity snatched a blanket off the bed, flung it over the child and rolled it away from the stove, which was now beginning to blaze fiercely. Very soon the whole place would be in flames and already the smoke was beginning to choke her. She hardly noticed the pain as she slapped out the flames on the child's clothing; even through her thick gloves she felt the sting of fire. She picked the child up, laid it gently in the cot and went to the window and took a deep breath. This time her screams for help were heard; kindly people from the sur-rounding houses came running into the street and moments later feet pounded up the stairs and two young men came blundering through the smoke.

Charity wasted no time in talk; she thrust the child into a pair of arms, snatched the baby from the cot and gave it to his companion. 'Quick,' she shouted at them, quite forgetting that she wasn't speaking their language, 'get out...'

It was a situation where words were unnecessary; they disappeared down the stairs and she tumbled down after them, her teeth chattering with fright. Outside a small crowd had gathered. 'Ambulance,' said Charity, and then began desperate attempts at Dutch. *'Ziekenwagen,'* she said urgently. 'Doctor, *Ziekenhuis*,' and, stumped for the words, 'Fire Brigade.' While she shouted all this she was taking a look at the children. The baby was a nasty bluish white but untouched by the fire. Charity gave it to a competent motherly-looking woman standing by. It was alive but it would need urgent treatment. As for the toddler, a little girl, she was severely burned but mercifully unconscious. Someone spoke to her but she couldn't understand a word, all she could do was repeat *'Ziekenhuis'* loudly and then, hopefully, *'Politie.'*

They arrived just as she was repeating another despairing cry for speedy help. A small car with two thickset, reassuringly calm policemen inside. Everyone spoke at once, but, calmly, Charity, terrified that the children would die unless they were helped quickly, cut through the din.

'The hospital,' she bawled at them, 'and do be quick, for heaven's sake.'

'English?' asked one of the policemen. 'The ambulance comes, also the fire engine . . .' As he spoke the ambulance arrived and, hard on its heels, the fire engine. The house was well alight by now but Charity could think only of the small creatures being loaded carefully into the ambulance. It drove away quickly and one of the policemen went around telling everyone in the small crowd to move along please—in Dutch, of course, but there was no mistaking it. She stood, rather at a loss, feeling a bit sick from the smoke and her fright and was rather surprised when the two men who had carried the children to safety, and had been talking to the policemen, came and shook her hand. The Dutch, she discovered, liked to shake hands a lot. She smiled and winced as hers were gripped and the scorched flesh under her gloves throbbed. Nothing much, she told herself, just the backs of her hands—not even her fingers—as one of the policemen came over to her.

'You will tell me, please, how this happened?'

It was a relief that he spoke English and understood it too. She gave him a businesslike account. 'And these two young men were so quick,' she finished. 'I hope that someone thanks them.'

'They will be thanked, miss. And you? You are OK? You were also quick. I wish for your name, please. You are a tourist?'

'No I work here...' She told him of her job at the hospital. 'It's my day off.'

'You wish to go there now?' He smiled in a fatherly fashion. 'You are dirty from the smoke and your coat is a little burnt.'

It seemed the sensible thing to do. 'Well, yes, I expect I'd better.'

Then he said, 'We will take you. It is possible that we shall wish to see you—perhaps tomorrow? At the hospital?'

She nodded. 'I work in the burns unit...'

They ushered her with clumsy care into the car as though she might fall apart at any moment, and they had good reason; her face was chalk-white, covered in greasy, sooty smoke, her coat was peppered by small burn marks where hot sparks had fallen upon it, and her hands were shaking so much that she had clutched them together, aware that they were painful but unable to do anything about it.

There was still a good deal of confusion; the firemen were getting the fire under control, the small crowd had rearranged itself, melting away when told to move on and then edging forward again.

'The parents?' asked Charity. 'Where are they?'

One of the constables spoke soothingly. 'They will be found, miss—we have information from the neighbours.'

'And the two men? Were they burnt?'

'No, no—just the smoke and that not much. They go also to the hospital.' He turned in his seat to smile at her. 'All is well, miss.'

She nodded, struggling with the urge to burst into tears, and minutes later they were at the hospital.

'*Eerstehulp*—we take you there...'

'Oh, please, no, If you would stop here I can go to the nurses' home...'

'There is someone to attend to you?'

'Yes, oh, yes. Thank you both so very much. I'll be here if you want me, tomorrow.'

The fatherly constable got out of the car and walked with her to the entrance, where he opened the door for her, patted her reassuringly on the back with a great hand like a ham, and waited until she had skimmed across the hall and disappeared down the corridor.

In the car again he said, 'We had better go and see how the little ones are.' When they had driven the short distance to the other department of the hospital, he spoke briefly on the car phone and then got out with his companion.

The baby had been borne away to the resuscitation room, and Professor van der Brons, called from his ward round, was bending over the toddler, not pausing in his careful examination when he was told that the police were there.

He questioned them closely without pausing in his work. 'She pulled the oil stove over,' he observed, 'poor little one. She is severely burned; did you get her out?'

The fatherly constable explained. 'This English girl was passing, went inside and put out the flames—two boys heard her screams and went to help her...'

'An English girl? Was she injured?'

'She said not, though her clothes were ruined. We took her back to the nurses' home a few minutes ago...'

The professor was gently lifting shreds of the child's clothing away from the burns with fine forceps. 'Zuster here will give you all the details you will want; we must get this child to the burns unit without delay.'

The toddler remained unconscious so that he could work on the small thin body without hindrance. They were very severe burns and even if she recovered the scars would be deep; she would need to come back time after time for skin grafts. He continued his painstaking work while his registrar attended to the plasma drip, making an occasional remark from time to time, his face calm and unworried, not allowing his thoughts to stray for one moment from the desperately ill child. At length he straightened up. 'Good, let us get her up to Theatre. Get this cleaned up and dressed before she rouses. We will keep her sedated but I want her specialled for the next forty-eight hours.' He glanced at his registrar. 'See to that, will you, Wim?'

He turned away while a nurse took his gown. 'Get another plasma up before we start, please. I'll want the theatre in fifteen minutes.'

He walked away, taking the phone from inside his pocket as he did so. By the time he reached the nurses' home, the warden was waiting for him.

He greeted her in his usual calm way. 'Zuster Charity Pearson—she has just returned here; she has been involved in a fire in the Jordaan. If you will come with me? She works on the burns unit and I wish to make sure that she is unhurt, Zuster Hengstma.'

The warden was a homely body, rather stout and inclined to gossip, but she was a motherly soul. 'The poor child. I've not seen her, Professor, or, depend upon it, I would have made sure...'

'Of course you would.' He smiled down at her. 'But I think we had better take a look, don't you?'

They went up in the lift to the third floor where Charity had a room, the warden looking worried, the professor his usual bland self.

Charity, having gained her room without being seen, had sat down on her bed and hadn't moved since. She still wore the coat, which smelled of burnt cloth and oil, and she hadn't taken off her gloves. She realised that she was in a mild state of shock, for her teeth chattered still and she couldn't stop shivering. She sat there, telling herself to get out of her clothes, have a warm bath, make a cup of tea and then get into bed and have a nap, all sensible things to do, and later, her old self again, she would go along to the warden and beg some mild treatment for her scorched hands.

However, her body refused to obey her; she just went on sitting there with no interest in what should happen next.

She didn't hear the warden's gentle tap on her door; it wasn't until it was opened and the warden entered, with Mr van der Brons looming behind her, that she looked up. The sight of his vast reassuring figure was too much for Charity; she burst into tears.

Zuster Hengstma trotted to her, making soothing clucking sounds and put her arms about her. Her English, always fragmental, gave way to a flood of Dutch, but what she was saying would have sounded kind in any language. Charity buried her face into the kind soul's ample bosom and sobbed.

Mr van der Brons said nothing at all, only sat himself down on the rather flimsy seat and waited patiently. Presently Charity's sobs became watery snorts and sniffs and he got up then, handed her a large, snowy handkerchief and sat down on the other side of her.

'We will have that coat off for a start,' he suggested mildly, 'and the gloves.' He viewed the ruin of her woolly cap atop the chaos of her hair. 'And the cap.'

She gave a prodigious sniff. 'So sorry,' she muttered. 'So silly of me to sit here like this. I'm quite all right, you know, just dirty.'

He didn't answer but smiled and nodded at the warden, who removed the cap and began to unbutton the coat, while he picked up first one hand and then the other and very gently drew off the gloves. She had been lucky; save for first-degree burns on the backs of her hands, she had escaped unhurt, although they were painful. He examined them carefully and put them back in her lap. 'We won't bother you with a lot of questions now,' he told her, with an impersonal kindness which she found soothing. 'Zuster Hengstma is going to help you to undress and have a bath and get you into bed and I will return and see to your hands. Not badly damaged, I'm glad to say, but they must be treated and you must have something for the pain.'

'I'm on duty in the morning . . .'

'No. You will have a day off. If you feel all right you may return on the following day, but only to light duties.' As she opened her mouth to protest, he said, 'No, no arguing.'

He got off the bed and went to the door and had a low-voiced conversation with the warden, then turned round to say, 'You are a very brave girl, Charity; we are all proud of you.'

Which for some reason started off the tears again.

An hour later she was sitting up in bed; Zuster Hengstma had bathed her despite her protests, washed her hair and anointed her face liberally with a nourishing cream. Mr van der Brons, ushered in with the deference due to a senior consultant, reflected that a shiny face and still damp brown hair were hardly aids to female beauty, and yet Charity managed to look decidedly—not pretty, he conceded, more like a child who had just been got ready for bed. He dismissed the thought as nonsense and listened composedly to Zuster Hengstma's recital of Charity's injuries.

She had got off lightly, he told her her; her scorched hands would heal in no time at all, and the scratches and bruises she had sustained would disappear within a few days.

'The baby?' she wanted to know. 'And the little girl? Are they going to be all right?'

'The baby is in the paediatric unit; it's early days yet . . . and the little girl is with us; early days for her too, but children are very resilient. I think that she has a very good chance—thanks to you—and she will of course have to come back from time to time for skin grafts.'

'Their mother and father. . .'

'The father was at work; the mother had gone down the street to get food.' He saw the look on her face and went on kindly, 'Don't condemn her, Charity. Will she not have to live with it for the rest of her life?'

'No no, I won't, only it's so sad,'

'It could have been even sadder.'

He went away presently, bidding her eat her late lunch like a good girl and take a nap afterwards.

She ate the lunch Zuster Hengstma brought to her but she had no intention of going to sleep. Lying in bed on her day off was a complete waste of time; she would go along to the nurses sitting-room and see what was on TV. She pushed the tray to one side and lay thinking about the rest of her day. When the warden slipped into the room ten minutes or so later Charity was asleep.

She was still asleep when the professor came to take another look at her. He nodded his satisfaction, handed the flowers he had brought to Zuster Hengstma and left a pile of magazines and books on the bedside table.

'Just keep her in bed for breakfast,' he suggested. 'She can get up and dress during the morning. I'll be along to see her about noon.'

The *directrice* had accompanied him this time, a stern-visaged lady with a heart of gold which was never allowed to show. She stood looking down at Charity, lying there with her hair all over the pillow, her mouth slightly open, her poor scorched hands lying neatly on the coverlet.

'We must let her see that we appreciate her bravery, Professor.'

'Indeed we must. If she is fit tomorrow I shall take her out to lunch.' He ignored her sharp look. 'And is there any way in which her clothes can be replaced? Could you suggest that she is covered by insurance or something similar?'

The *directrice*'s stern mouth twitched. 'I'm sure that I can think of something, Mr van der Brons.'

They went away together and when Charity awoke it was to see Zuster Hengstma standing by the bed with the tea tray.

'The professor came again,' explained that lady. 'He has brought you flowers and books and after tea you may have visitors.'

The flowers were beautiful and the books would keep her happy for hours. And visitors... She wondered just for a moment if Cor would come and see her and then dismissed the thought.

Of course he didn't, but several of the nurses came, eager to hear all about the fire and her part in it, being friendly and kind and talking a lot so that by the time she had had her supper she was ready for bed again. She lay back against the extra pillows the warden had brought for her, dipping into the books and glancing every now and then at the vase of lilac, carnations, roses and freesias on the dressing table. Mr van der Brons was really very kind, she thought sleepily: he didn't say much but somehow he didn't need to; he was the kind of person one could confide in without feeling a fool. She began to wonder what kind of life he led away from the hospital. It would be interesting to know, but she thought it unlikely that she ever would; he wasn't a talkative man and to try to find out about him from other people seemed sneaky.

She put down the books and turned off the bedside light. When she saw him again on duty she must thank him for his kindness. He must have been thinking of his sister in Edinburgh, she thought sleepily, a little muddled in the head, but knowing exactly what she meant.

She closed her eyes and thought about the next day; she had been told to stay in bed for breakfast but after that she would go out and buy a new coat. Grey or brown, she debated, useful colours which would go with everything she had; she would have to spend the money she had earmarked for a dress and boots. It was her last waking, regretful thought.

CHAPTER THREE

EXCEPT for the backs of her hands, Charity felt quite herself when she woke up the following morning. Having breakfast brought to her in her bed seemed quite unnecessary, but a treat she had seldom enjoyed. Zuster Hengstma fussed around her, chattering away in Dutch just as though Charity understood every word, and, since she was a kind-hearted woman, Charity made no bones about trying out her own version of the Dutch language.

Zuster Hengstma patted her shoulder. 'Your Dutch is good,' she said not quite truthfully, 'and it will be better. Now you may get up if you wish. The *directrice* will come and see you later.'

So Charity dressed herself and settled down to read one of the books. When the *directrice* had been she would take herself off for the rest of the day, somewhere quiet; the Amsterdam Historic Museum would do nicely and one of the nurses had told her that there was a restaurant there—she could have a snack lunch before going in search of a new coat. Having decided what to do with the rest of her day, she opened the copy of *Jane Eyre* which Mr van der Brons had sent, reflecting that it was a happy surprise that the books were all very much to her taste.

The *directrice* came shortly after eleven o'clock, accompanied by Mr van der Brons, who wished her a civil good morning, hoped that she had slept well, gave her hands a quick look and then stood by the window, staring out at the wintry day, which gave the *directrice* an opportunity to enquire in her turn as to Charity's health.

'I am delighted that you were not more seriously hurt,' she told her, 'and I must commend you upon your courage and quick thinking. You have ruined your coat, I am told. Perhaps you do not know that our nurses are insured against mishap of any sort, so that within a short time you will receive a sum sufficient to replace what you have lost. In the meantime, if you present yourself at the secretary's office today or tomorrow an advance payment will be made so that you may purchase a coat without any delay.'

She glanced sideways at the professor, still absorbed in the view. 'Mr van der Brons will tell you when he thinks that you will be fit to resume work, Zuster Pearson, and I must repeat that we are all proud of you.' She smiled then. 'Now enjoy the rest of your day and do be careful.'

She sailed away, glancing at the professor as he opened the door for her. His nod was approving and almost imperceptible.

Charity was surprised when he turned back into her room. 'I am free for a few hours,' he observed casually. 'Perhaps you will have lunch with me? I have heard so many versions of yesterday's happenings that I should be glad to hear the facts from you.'

'Oh, would you? How are the children?'

'The little girl is coming along nicely, although we can't be sure of anything for a day or two. The baby is having chest trouble—only to be expected. He is in IT.' He added soothingly, 'Babies are very tough...' He smiled gently. 'And now what about that lunch?'

'I'd like to come very much, Mr van der Brons, but could it be somewhere where I can wear a raincoat?'

'No problem. I'll see you downstairs in half an hour and in the meantime I suggest that you go along to the secretary and get the money for a new coat.'

'Could I? It's not too soon? I mean, he will know?'

'Certainly, since the *directrice* seems to have arranged it.'

He sauntered away and she started the swift redoing of her face and hair, got into the raincoat and for lack of a hat tied a scarf under her chin. The only other gloves she had were woollen and not at all suitable for going out to lunch with one of the consultants, but there was nothing she could do about that. After lunch she would go and buy another pair, a coat too... which reminded her that she had been told to go to the secretary's office.

The hospital secretary was an important and rather formidable figure; she had only spoken to him once soon after her arrival at the hospital and although he had been very civil he had been distant.

When she tapped on his door he got up to wish her a good morning, made rather a gruff speech about her bravery and begged her to sit down. He had a paper before him on his desk which he asked her to sign.

'If you will take my word for it that this is merely a receipt for the money you are about to receive, so that it may be passed to the insurers.'

He had handed her a pen and she had signed and then rather late in the day asked, 'I shan't have to pay this money back?'

'No, certainly not. This is the money due to you for the loss of your coat and any other garment which has been damaged.' He handed her a bundle of notes and said, 'Please count them.'

She counted and then said, 'Heavens above, I could buy two coats with this.'

'Clothes are expensive here in Holland. I can assure you that you are entitled to every cent which is here.'

He got up to open the door for her and she went along to the entrance, doing sums in her head—there was enough to buy a good coat, gloves, a hat, a dress... The professor, watching her crossing the entrance hall, smiled a little at the rapt expression on her face. He had seen the same look on his sisters' faces when they were planning a shopping expedition.

Driving away from the hospital, the professor said blandly, 'I suspect that you are still fussing about your clothes—there is no need; we are lunching at my home.'

She turned a surprised face to his, but he was looking ahead. She was forced to address his profile. 'Your home? But I can't, that is, I haven't met your wife—she might not——'

'I'm not married, or, rather, I have been married; my wife died ten years ago.'

'I'm sorry. Have you any children?'

'Two daughters, ten-year-old twins.'

Charity did some mental arithmetic. 'Oh, they don't remember their mother?'

'Hardly.' His voice was dry. 'She left us when they were six months old. She and the man she had gone to live with were killed in a car accident very shortly afterwards.'

'That's awful... I'm so sorry, how terrible for you— and for them, you must miss...' She was aware that she was babbling, and then she said, 'Thank you for telling me.'

He didn't answer, but he turned the car into a narrow street lined with gabled houses and stopped before one of them, got out, opened the door of the car and ushered her across the narrow pavement and up the double steps to his front door, a massive affair of splendid wood with a solid brass knocker. He unlocked it and pushed her gently ahead of him into a small vestibule with an inner door which was opened as they reached it by Jolly, who, if he was surprised at the sight of Charity, allowed none of it to show, but murmured politely, took her raincoat and hurried to open the double doors on one side of the hall.

Before she reached them Charity was able to cast a quick eye around her. The hall was panelled in dark oak, shoulder-high, and above it there was a crimson wallpaper; the floor was black and white marble and a Delft china and brass chandelier hung from the ceiling. That was all she had time to notice before going past Jolly into a magnificent room which overlooked the street. It had a high ceiling of strapwork and a splendid chimney-piece of some gleaming golden wood above a wide hearth in which a fire burned briskly. Its two long windows were framed by crimson velvet curtains and elaborate pelmets. There were soft rugs strewn on the polished wood floor and two large sofas on each side of the fireplace. There were great armchairs too and a William and Mary settee covered in worn tapestry as well as lamp tables and an enormous bow-fronted display cabinet along one wall. Very grand but lived-in too, she decided, catching sight of the dog Samson, who had advanced to meet them, and a very ordinary tabby cat stretched out before the fire.

'Sit down,' invited Mr van der Brons. 'There is just time for a drink before lunch. Letizia and Teile will be here in a few minutes.'

He sat himself down near her and began a rambling conversation calculated to put her at her ease until the door opened and the two little girls came in. They were identical twins with their father's blue eyes and flaxen hair cut into fringes across their wide foreheads; they wore kilts and jumpers, obviously expensive but far too sombre in colour.

It was at once evident that they had a splendid rapport with their father; they swarmed over him, chattering endlessly until he hushed them. 'I've brought someone home for lunch,' he told them in English. 'This is Charity Pearson; she works with me at the hospital and she comes from England.'

They came to shake her hand and bid her 'How do you do' in English, and at her look of surprise the professor observed, 'They have an English governess; unfortunately she has to go back to her home to look after her mother. We shall miss her. I hope you will meet her before she goes; we are all fond of her.'

'Do you go to school?' Charity asked a twin, uncertain which one it was.

'Yes, we are in the same class. We're clever.'

'That is enough of that, Teile,' said the professor firmly. 'Charity is a clever young lady who doesn't boast about it.'

'Are you clever?' asked Teile.

Charity cast Mr van der Brons a reproachful glance. 'I can knit and sew and cook, and make things from cardboard and paper.'

'What sort of things?' asked Letizia,

'Boxes to put things in and dolls, and I make dolls' clothes and houses, but the house was a bit difficult.'

The little girls looked at her with admiration. 'So you are clever. We'd like to make a dolls' house...' they exchanged glances '...but Miss Bloom won't let us do anything that requires no effort of our brains.'

Charity had the lowering feeling that she wouldn't match up to Miss Bloom's high standards; it helped a little when Mr van der Brons said in his most soothing voice, 'She is enjoying a day off.' Charity's sigh of relief was barely discernible.

Jolly came then to tell them that lunch was ready and they crossed the hall, with Samson close at his master's heels, and entered the dining-room on the other side of the hall. It was panelled in dark oak just as the hall was, with white-plastered walls above, hung with paintings. It had a splendid strapwork ceiling, an enormous carved sideboard along one wall, a massive dining table ringed by ladderback chairs, and another display cabinet. Yet, Charity reflected, it had the pleasant air of being lived in. The furniture might be priceless museum pieces but this was no museum, it was a home.

The meal was a lively one—not that Mr van der Brons was anything other than his usual placid self, but the two little girls chattered happily enough as they ate their omelettes and salad, plying Charity with questions about her work. 'Where do you live—and where is home?' asked Letizia.

'Well, when I'm in London I live at the hospital——'

'But your home? Where is that?'

Charity considered that it was time the professor halted the stream of questions but he said nothing, sitting there, smiling a little. She cast him a cross look and said, 'I haven't a home; you see, I have no family.'

'Have some of ours,' offered Mr van der Brons lazily. 'We have more brothers and sisters, aunts and uncles, grannies and cousins than I care to count.'

The little girls shrieked with laughter. After a moment Charity laughed too; it was impossible not to in the face of her host's placid good humour.

They all went back into the drawing-room presently and played Monopoly until the afternoon darkened and Charity looked guiltily at the clock and saw what time it was.

'I must go!' she exclaimed. 'It's almost four o'clock—I forgot the time...'

'This is a game to make one forget everything, even the time,' observed Mr van der Brons, 'but of course you can't go without your tea.' He smiled at her. 'I would have invited you to stay for dinner but unfortunately I have a date and these two go to bed at half-past seven.'

Teile had got off her chair and was standing beside her father, one arm round his neck. 'Papa, please don't go out; if you stayed then Charity could stay too.'

'*Liefje,* I cannot break an engagement with a lady.'

'Is it that Mevrouw de Groot?'

'It is.' Her father's voice held a steely note and Teile subsided into a silence which Charity broke before it began to be awkward.

'I'm going to the cinema this evening,' she fibbed hurriedly, 'with some of the nurses. I've forgotten the name of the film but it's an American one. I haven't been to a cinema since I got here.'

She looked up and found the professor's sleepy eyes on her. He didn't believe a word but the little girls did. The conversation became animated over a discussion about the cinema and the films they had seen and lasted nicely until Jolly came in with the tea. Proper afternoon tea, Charity was glad to see, little dainty sandwiches and scones and a large fruit cake, and the teapot—a splendid example of Georgian silver—was a family size and contained reassuringly strong tea, a nice change from the weak straw-coloured tea which was served at the hospital.

'I have it sent over from Fortnum and Mason,' observed Mr van der Brons, reading her tell-tale expression. 'Be mother, will you, Charity? Teile and Letizia have a watered-down version.'

So they had a pleasant tea, although Charity kept an anxious eye on the clock, keen not to outstay her welcome.

When the small meal was finished she said in her matter-of-fact way, 'I think I must go, if you don't mind . . .'

'Ah, yes, the cinema; we mustn't keep you. What a pleasant hour or so we have spent, not, I hope, too dull for you?'

'Dull?' She was astonished at his question. 'How could it possibly be dull? I've loved every minute of it.' And, in case that sounded too enthusiastic, she added, 'It was lovely meeting your little girls.'

She beamed at Teile and Letizia, who grinned back at her.

'Come again?' they begged, and she murmured vaguely because Mr van der Brons hadn't added his voice to theirs. 'It would be fun to make a dolls' house,' said Teile wistfully.

'Oh, but I dare say you have one,' said Charity bracingly.

'Well, of course we have. We didn't make it, though—there's a difference...'

Charity agreed that there was, submitted to protracted embraces, was helped into her coat and went into the cold evening with the professor. They drove back to the hospital in silence and when they reached its entrance she embarked on her speech of thanks to be interrupted by his, 'I'm coming in—I've a patient to see.'

They walked together into the entrance and halfway across it she stopped. 'Thank you for a lovely day,' she told him earnestly, 'and I like your daughters.'

He stood looking down at her, not smiling. 'They liked you, Charity. Tell me, do you like me?'

She smiled widely at him. 'Oh, yes, indeed, I do—you're—you're safe, if you see what I mean?'

His expression didn't alter. 'You mean that I'm not another van Kamp to make havoc of your heart,' he said evenly.

She nodded. 'Yes.'

'Does he still do that?'

She thought for a moment. 'Well, just now and then. But I'll not... That is, I've learnt my lesson.'

'You don't wish to go back to England?'

'Certainly not. I like it here and I like working on your unit; besides, that would be running away.'

'Indeed it would. I am pleased to know that you like your work. You will, of course, be on light duties tomorrow. Sister will tell you exactly what you may and may not do.'

She said awkwardly, 'Yes, of course, Professor. Good evening.'

She had kept him standing there, she thought worriedly, boring him stiff, probably, when all he wanted to do was to see his patient. She would have to take care to let him see that she had no intention of taking advantage of his kindness.

She had no need to do that during the next few days for she saw almost nothing of him and then only briefly when he came to visit patients waiting for skin grafts or those on the point of being discharged. Her hands gave her no pain but they were beginning to peel and Zuster Kingsma wouldn't allow her anywhere near patients who had just received their skin grafts or those who had been admitted as emergencies. So she made beds, helped convalescent patients to pack their things ready to go home, turned out cupboards and kept well away from the busy heart of the unit.

A week went by and she had a day off once more. She went off duty in the evening, intent on her plans. She was poring over a train timetable in the nurses' sitting-room when the warden put her head round the door.

'For you,' she said, nodding at Charity. 'There is a telephone call.'

'Me? I don't know anyone...' She followed the warden out of the room. It could be Eunice, in Amsterdam, perhaps on a modelling job. She picked up the receiver and said 'Hello,' in an enquiring voice.

'I shall be outside at half-past eight,' said Mr van der Brons in her ear. 'Please don't keep me waiting.' When she didn't answer he said, 'You are still planning to go to Leiden tomorrow, are you not?'

'Yes, yes, I am but I can go by train, you know.'

'Yes, I do know. If I remember rightly, though, I offered you a lift.'

'Yes, you did, only I didn't know that you were still going or—or if you had forgotten or anything.'

'I had not forgotten. I will see you in the morning.'

He rang off, leaving her faintly put out at his abrupt finish. Of course she could make some excuse, leave a message at the porter's lodge, but that would look a bit silly. She would accept his offer of a lift; after all, it was a short journey to Leiden and she would be careful to keep the conversation casual and especially remember not to talk about herself.

She went to her room and reviewed her scanty wardrobe. There hadn't been time to go shopping for a new coat and she had decided to go to Leiden and put off its buying until her next day off. Now it was too late to do anything about that. It would have to be the raincoat again and the unsuitable shoes. She had enough money now to get a new outfit and since she would have all day in Leiden she decided to go round the shops there. A coat, she mused, boots, a cap, or something to wear in the cold weather, perhaps even a dress. She suddenly felt quite cheerful at the prospect of new clothes.

As it turned out, it was raining so hard in the morning that anything other than a raincoat would have been useless. It was another matter with the shoes but they looked fairly sensible in spite of the fact that they were no longer watertight.

Mr van der Brons was outside in his car but he got out, seemingly oblivious to the weather, to open her door. 'Not much of a day,' he observed cheerfully. His eye swept carelessly over the shoes. 'Fortunately there is a good deal to see in Leiden; the Lakenhal is well worth a visit and of course Sint Pieterskerk and the museum of Antiquities on the Rapenburg. Then there is the Ethnographical Museum and the History of Science Museum—they're close together. I thought we might have lunch together. There's a *pannekoekenhuis* in the centre of the town. If you feel like it I'll be there by half-past twelve. I have some consultations in the afternoon, but if you can find your way down Rapenburg to the medical school you'll see the car. About five o'clock. Will you wait in the university entrance if I'm not there?'

There seemed no point in refusing and anyway she couldn't think of a way to do it without sounding rude. She thanked him in her quiet voice and made a colourless remark about the weather. He followed her lead, agreeing placidly that the weather in Holland was frequently wet and windy, enlarging upon this dull topic until the subject had been wrung dry. It was a good thing that the journey to Leiden was a short one. He stopped briefly outside the Lakenhal, advised her to have a cup of coffee at a small café nearby until its doors were open, and drove off.

Since it was still raining she took his advice and then, as it was still too early to visit the Lakenhal, she took herself off to the shopping streets. She was agreeably surprised to find that although they were smaller and fewer than those in Amsterdam they displayed some very attractive clothes. Much taken by a dark green coat, well cut and not too expensive, she opened the shop door and went inside, intent on trying it on. It fitted, what was more it suited her, and the saleswoman, whose English was a great deal better than Charity's Dutch, pointed out that she had just the right hat to go with it; felt with a small brim, which she perched on Charity's tidy head at just the right angle. Charity agreed that it seemed a shame not to buy it as it was such a splendid match and from that it was an easy step to glancing through a selection of dresses to complete the outfit. Separates, said the saleswoman, in a fine wool; she had just the thing in a green and tawny Paisley pattern, or perhaps the cranberry needlecord? Charity, after deliberation, decided on the needlecord. The coat and hat were put on once more just to make sure that the whole ensemble was exactly to her liking and since it had stopped raining she kept them on, paid her bill and went outside into the street again. There were more people about now and the Lakenhal would have opened its doors but Charity, quite carried away by her smart appearance, studied the shoe shops, weighing the variety of boots against each other and finally settling on a pair of soft leather boots—black, for her handbag was black and, being leather, was still good. Once again, she emerged, her feet newly shod, the unsuitable shoes sharing the bag into which her raincoat had been packed.

The sun had come out too; she made her way jauntily to the Lakenhal and spent an hour there before walking down Breestraat to study the Town Hall, the Korenbeursbrug and then Burcht Fort, St Pancras Church and finally breasting the hill to the Sint Pieterkerk. By then it was very nearly half-past twelve, so she retraced her steps, found Steenstraat, and, in it, the *pannekoekenhuis*.

Mr van der Brons was already there although she didn't see him at once. He stood a little to one side, watching her coming towards him. He smiled a little at the new clothes but it was a kind smile and as she got nearer he came towards her, his smile casually friendly now.

He took her plastic bag from her and said, 'I see you have put your morning to good advantage. You look very nice. Did you find time to visit any of the museums or to look round the town?'

His voice held just the right tone of casual interest as he ushered her into the restaurant, sat her down at a table by a window and took off his car coat. 'I hope you are hungry, for I am. Have you had a Dutch pancake yet?'

When she shook her head he said, 'Then that's what we will have, *spekpannenkoeken* with *stroop*—fat bacon pancakes with syrup.'

'Shall I like it?' She did sound rather doubtful.

'Most certainly you will. Let me have that coat.'

He handed it to a waiter and ordered the pancakes. 'I won't offer you lager—would you like wine or tonic?'

She chose tonic water and over their drinks she told him, remembering to be brief, of her morning. The pancakes came then so that conversation was spasmodic. They had almost finished when he asked her, 'Did you enjoy that?'

'Very much. It doesn't sound nearly as nice as it tastes.'

'Good. Shall we have coffee?' and, when it came, 'What do you intend to do this afternoon?'

'Well, I haven't seen the Rapenburg Canal yet and there are some gardens, aren't there? I don't suppose there's much to see at this time of year, but I thought I would take a look.'

'Then there are always the shops,' he reminded her smilingly.

His manners were far too good to remind her that he had work to do that afternoon; she drank her coffee and said, 'Yes, I'll do the rest of my shopping before I start to explore.'

She got up, he helped her into her coat and they went together into the street. 'Thank you for my lunch,' said Charity. 'I'll not be late.'

He smiled down at her earnest face, quite pretty now by reason of the new clothes and the pleasure of his company. 'I'll wait, Charity.'

She gave him rather a shy smile and walked away briskly in the direction of the shops, and, although he was already a little late for his appointment, he stood watching her until she was out of sight.

Charity still had some money in her purse; she spent most of it during the next hour, on undies and tights, a pretty scarf, a night cream guaranteed to bring beauty to the plainest face, a new lipstick. She called a halt then and spent a sober hour at the History of Science Museum, going out of her way to understand its contents before making her way to the Rapenburg Canal and having tea in the Doelen Restaurant, where she dawdled over a pot of tea and an outsize cream cake, and by then it was time to go across the canal and look for the Rolls.

It was quite dark by now and cold but the town was brightly lit and in some of the houses there were lit Christmas trees. Despite the chilly air she loitered along, enjoying the last of her free day.

She paused going over the bridge to look down at the canal and the thought struck her that she hadn't remembered Cor once all day. Now, suddenly, she wished that he was there, standing beside her, his arm round her shoulders, talking light-heartedly, telling her that she was his girl and that there was no one like her. All nonsense, she reminded herself very firmly, but all the same hard to forget.

The professor, walking towards her, paused to study her; even from that distance he could see her straight little back drooping. He sighed gently and went on walking, making sufficient noise for her to turn to see who it was. Just for a moment she had the wild idea that it was Cor, so engrossed was she in thoughts of him, but it was Mr van der Brons who came unhurriedly to join her.

'Peaceful, isn't it?' he remarked without looking at her. 'I like to think of all the people who have stood on this bridge over the hundreds of years. One wonders if they were happy or unhappy, in love or at odds with everyone.'

He stood beside her, leaning against the parapet, and his calm voice matched the calm of their surroundings. Charity felt her sadness melting away and her good sense taking over once more. The future was ahead and heaven knew what was in store for her; in the meantime she had a good job and enough money now and the nurses at the hospital were friendly. She would stop being sorry for herself; she had been a fool but she had learnt her lesson.

'I had a look at the gardens,' she told him. 'I wish I knew more about the university—it's a big medical school, isn't it?'

He told her about it, standing there in the cold dark of the evening, his arm around her shoulders, until at length he paused. 'You must be frozen... You must have a warm drink before you go back. In any case, Letizia and Teile want to see you again.'

He didn't listen to her objections but swept her along and into the car and within half an hour she found herself in his house, having her new coat taken from her and being shooed gently into the drawing-room.

'Coffee,' said the professor, 'hot and strong while you defrost before the fire. Here come Teile and Letizia.'

The children came prancing in with Samson between them and before she knew where she was Charity was drinking Mevrouw Jolly's coffee, deep in a game of Scrabble. She did look up once to say, 'But I really must go...' This was met with his mild, 'Why? Have you something planned for this evening?' When she shook her head, he said slowly, 'Well, let us hear no more about it. You must stay to supper and fend off the children's endless questions.'

So she stayed, but it wasn't supper; it was an elegant dinner served on spotless linen and eaten with silver cutlery.

'We don't usually stay up as late as this,' explained Teile, 'only it's Saturday tomorrow and we don't go to school. Besides, Miss Bloom is coming back this evening; she had to go to England again.'

So when dinner was finished Charity said that she must go. 'You will want to talk to Miss Bloom,' she said in her matter-of-fact way. 'She will be so pleased to see you again.' She put down her coffee-cup and got to her feet, and the professor stood up and pushed her gently back into her chair. 'Miss Bloom will be delighted to meet you, Charity. I'm going to Schiphol to meet her plane now and I'm relying on you to stay here and keep an eye on the girls. I'll take you back...'

He so obviously took it for granted that she would agree to this that she nodded weakly. He patted her briskly on the shoulder, spoke to the little girls in their own language and left the room. Charity, feeling annoyed for no reason that she could think of, returned to their game of Scrabble.

It was nearly an hour before Mr van der Brons returned, this time accompanied by a severe-looking lady clad in equally severe tweeds, her greying hair drawn back into an old-fashioned bun. The little girls, who had been sprawling on the floor, got to their feet as she entered the room and went to offer her a polite greeting, and Charity, who had been sprawling too, scrambled to her feet, feeling guilty. The professor looked at her flushed face and untidy hair and smiled to himself, but he undertook the introductions with grave politeness and Charity and Miss Bloom shook hands, exchanging the polite remarks usual on such occasions. Then she said, 'It was a delightful surprise to be greeted by you both, Teile and Letizia, but it is long past your bedtime. Say goodnight to your Father and Miss Pearson and go upstairs.'

They kissed their father obediently and then, rather to her surprise, kissed Charity as well. When they had gone Miss Bloom observed, 'I shall miss them, you know—almost ten years is a long time...' She turned to Mr van der Brons. 'Have you a governess in mind?'

'Well, no. I am thinking of marrying, in which case there should be no need.' He smiled at her, then, 'I should never find anyone quite like you, Miss Bloom.'

Miss Bloom blushed. 'That is kind of you to say so, Mr van der Brons. I very much regret that I must return home as soon as possible. Probably before you marry?'

'Probably.

He wasn't going to say any more than that, and Charity filled the small silence with a reiterated wish to return to the hospital, a wish he agreed to with unflattering promptness. Getting into her coat, she reflected that probably he was free to spend the rest of the evening with whomever it was he was going to marry. She contemplated this gloomily, not sure why the sparkle had gone out of the day, but she bade Miss Bloom a cheerful goodbye, expressed her wish that that lady should enjoy her future and got into the car beside Mr van der Brons. The drive was so brief that there was really no need to say anything, but when he stopped before the hospital entrance she said, 'No, please don't get out—I'm sure you must have plans for your evening.'

He took no notice, but walked with her to the doors, where she thanked him for her delightful day. 'You'll miss Miss Bloom,' she ended, by way of finishing their brief conversation.

'Oh, yes, I must do something about that. Goodnight, Charity.'

CHAPTER FOUR

CHARITY went on duty the next morning, looking forward to seeing Mr van der Brons again. Probably he wouldn't speak to her—to be friends outside the hospital was one thing; in the unit she was Staff Nurse Pearson and he was the boss, however placidly he held that position—but just to see him would be nice...

He wasn't there. Zuster Kingsma, giving her instructions for the day, observed that he had been called away during the very early hours of the morning to do what he could for a badly burned child in an outlying village. There was no sign of him all day and she went off duty at half-past three, feeling disappointed. She had agreed to go with some of the other nurses to a cinema that evening; it was on their way back to the hospital, rattling along in one of Amsterdam's trams, that she saw him go past in his car. There was an elegant-looking woman beside him and for some reason the sight of them together annoyed Charity; the day, which had began so cheerfully, ended on a sour note.

In bed later, she took herself to task; it was not as though they were real friends, she reminded herself—each time she had been out with him it was really because, being a kind man, he wasn't able to do anything else. He had taken her out to cheer her up on the first occasion, hadn't he? Then he had offered a lift to Leiden also from kindness, and he had asked her to lunch at his home because she had been an object of pity in her ruined clothes. He wasn't likely to foster an acquaintance which had been foisted upon him in the first place.

She had the afternoon shift the next day and went on duty after her midday dinner to find that he had been in the unit the whole morning and had gone again, this time over to Edinburgh, where he expected to stay for several days. His registrar, Wim van Beek, said Zuster Kingsma, would deal with any emergency and minor surgery.

It was silly of her to miss him and even sillier to think of him so much; there were so many other things to think about—in two days' time it would be the feast of Sint Nikolaas and the other nurses had told her that it was usual to give friends and family some small gift. Especially the children. In the meantime she intended to roam around the shops, buying headscarves, hankies and scented soap for her widening circle of companions. It was a pity that the children on the ward were all too ill to enjoy presents—perhaps by Christmas...

Two days later it was her afternoon shift again and since it was Sint Nikolaas she took her presents on duty with her; the nursing staff had clubbed together and bought Zuster Kingsma a silk headscarf, traditionally labelled from the *sint,* as were the small packets for the nurses and those of the patients who were well enough to enjoy the mild pleasure of opening a parcel. It was a pity, Zuster Kingsma told her, that the feast of Sint Nikolaas was taking second place to Christmas; only the children still received small gifts and chocolate letters and gathered to see the *sint* and his attendant Zwarte Piet ride through the cities and towns of Holland. All the same, in the hospital small presents were exchanged among friends.

Charity went off duty that evening, clutching a chocolate letter and a handful of soaps, hankies and a coffee-mug. Even amid the hurry and bustle of the unit there had been time to exchange presents and to admire those brought in by family and friends of the patients who were well enough to enjoy them. It had been a very busy day and she was tired now. Supper, she thought, a hot bath and then bed.

She was crossing the entrance hall, using the corridor at its far end as so many of the nurses did, even though it was forbidden, since it was the shortest route to the nurses' home, when she saw Mr van der Brons's broad back disappearing through the entrance doors. He was back, she thought contentedly, and she would see him in the morning.

Early though it was, he was in Sister's office when she went on duty in the morning. Beyond his usual courteous good morning he had nothing to say to her, but at the door he paused to speak to Zuster Kingsma in English. 'I'll have Zuster Pearson in Theatre this morning; arrange that, if you please.'

Zuster Kingsma waited until he had gone. 'A good morning for your first in Theatre,' she said kindly. 'First stage pedicle and a first dressing on that child we admitted—under anaesthetic.'

Theatre Sister was small and round with black eyes and a placid face and, mindful of Mr van der Brons's instructions, she took care that Charity stayed in the background so that she had time to find her feet and undertake only the simplest of tasks. Mr van der Brons, looming large over everyone else, was assisted by his registrar and two young housemen, who got very much in the way and whom he treated with great patience, explaining just what he was doing and why and encouraging them to air their views. Most of it was lost on Charity, for he spoke Dutch, but from time to time Sister spoke to her in English, bidding her do something or other, and she understood well enough when one or other of the nurses there said something to her. By the end of the morning she had lost her initial nervousness and, when the list was finished, did her share of cleaning up and readying the theatre for any emergency which might happen.

Mr van der Brons had gone again, of course, without so much as glancing her way. It couldn't be plainer, she thought sadly; he had helped her when she had needed help and that was that. Not surprising, she reminded herself, tearing out of her uniform later that afternoon, intent on getting to the shops to look for Christmas presents; now if it had been Eunice with her lovely face and beguiling ways it might have been a different matter...

She was surprised to have a letter from Miss Bloom the following morning, suggesting that they might meet for tea on her next free afternoon. It was a stiff little note but she had written her telephone number and hoped that Charity would meet her, suggesting the Bijenkorf restaurant at four o'clock.

Charity was intrigued; she had thought Miss Bloom a little intimidating but there must be something nice about her for her to have stayed with the van der Bronses for so many years. She phoned during her coffee break and arranged to meet her that very afternoon.

It was rather a scramble to get to the Bijenkorf by four o'clock; clock-watching wasn't encouraged on the burns unit and in any case Charity wasn't a clock-watcher. Doubtless Miss Bloom wouldn't mind waiting for ten minutes or so.

She arrived rather breathless, a little late but as neat as a new pin. 'I'm late,' she apologised. 'I'm so sorry, but Mr van der Brons was doing a round and we are all expected to stay until it is over.'

Miss Bloom, unmistakably English in a tweed coat of a timeless cut, a sensible felt hat pulled well down, sensible lace-up shoes and gloves and handbag which must have cost more than the whole of the rest of her outfit, was sitting at a table for two overlooking the shop floor below. She shook hands and said, 'I ordered tea and toast. I hope that will suit you?' Charity said that it would, stifling greedy thoughts of mountainous cream cakes.

'We met only briefly the other evening,' said Miss Bloom, 'and it has occurred to me that since I have lived here for some years and you are newly arrived there might be some way in which I could help you.'

'You're very kind. I've been here almost three months and I'm beginning to find my way around and learn some Dutch, but there's so much I don't know.'

'You should find someone to give you lessons—does the hospital arrange that?'

'Oh, yes—but the teacher has too big a class already; I'm to join after Christmas.'

Their tea came and Miss Bloom poured out and offered buttered toast; Charity, who had had a curtailed midday dinner, could have wolfed the lot. She nibbled at a thin slice and responded politely to Miss Bloom's chat.

They were enjoying their second cups when Miss Bloom observed, 'You are a most fortunate girl to be working for Mr van der Brons. He is a kind and generous man and endlessly patient.'

Charity agreed. 'He has been very kind to me—I imagine he's nice to everyone.'

'Yes, although of course if he comes across injustice or unkindness he can exhibit a quite royal rage. He will, however, go out of his way to help anyone who needs it.'

This was a little near the bone for Charity. She said cheerfully, 'I liked his daughters...'

'Dear girls; they take after him and I am glad to say that they are not like their mother.' She turned a shrewd eye upon Charity. 'He was good enough to tell me of your bravery. It is a wonder that you weren't more severely injured.'

Charity went a little pink. 'I don't think I was in any real danger and those two young men who came after us were awfully quick.'

'You were quicker.' Miss Bloom smiled warmly and Charity discovered that she rather liked her after all. 'I return to England in two weeks. I hope that you will see something of Teile and Letizia—they liked you.'

'Well, I don't suppose that's very likely. I mean, I don't know Mr van der Brons, if you see what I mean. I work on his unit—it's...it's not quite the same.' She added in her matter-of-fact way, 'I'm sure he must have lots of friends.' She was suddenly anxious not to talk about him any more. 'You will be sorry to go back to England?'

'Oh, yes. But my mother is ill—a bad heart which will, I'm afraid, deteriorate. I must make my home with her.'

'Later on, if your mother should improve, you could perhaps return—the girls will miss you dreadfully after all these years...'

'I like to think so. I shall do my best to keep in contact with them.'

They decided on a third cup of tea and she went on, 'Are you looking forward to Christmas?'

They chatted for a little while longer before Charity said that she must go if she was to do her shopping before closing time. She thanked Miss Bloom and hoped that they might meet again some time. 'For I shall return to England, I expect, although I like Holland very much, what I've seen of it.'

They parted on the most friendly terms and Charity, buying Christmas cards, wondered why Miss Bloom had wanted to meet her again and then forgot about it as she wandered through the Bijenkorf's departments.

Mr van der Brons let himself into his house very much later that evening. He declined Jolly's offer of a meal and went into his drawing-room to find Miss Bloom sitting there, knitting. Samson came to greet him and he bent to caress the dog's shaggy coat. 'Good evening, Miss Bloom,' he said pleasantly, and went to sit down in his great arm-chair by the fire, not allowing his surprise at seeing her there to show. She was an old and trusted member of his household, but although they shared their meals when he was at home and from time to time discussed the children's problems and progress she had her own sitting-room and only rarely sought him out.

'You are wondering why I am here, Mr van der Brons.' Miss Bloom wasn't a woman to beat about the bush. 'But I have something to ask of you while Teile and Letizia are not with us. Today I had tea with Miss Pearson—such a nice girl—and I cannot help but think that it might be of benefit to the children if they were to see more of her—make her their friend. She is young enough to enjoy their company yet old enough to exert some authority. They will miss me for a time and she will soften the blow. I observed her carefully as we had tea and I was impressed by her quiet manner—and her voice is charming. They like her, as you know, and have several times wished to meet her again. I realise that you can hardly encroach on her work and life at the hospital. I should imagine that she would have friends there, but perhaps once in a while she could meet the girls?'

Mr van der Brons was sitting back in his chair, his eyes half closed, his face expressing nothing more than placid interest.

'An excellent idea, Miss Bloom. I formed a good opinion of Miss Pearson when I first met her and I have observed her at the hospital—she could never fill your shoes but she might, as you say, help the girls over a difficult time when you leave us.'

Miss Bloom folded her knitting and put it away neatly into a large bag. 'Then you would have no objection if I were to ask her to tea again and take the children with me?'

'None at all. Better still, invite her here—they won't need to be on their best behaviour then and they'll get to know each other better.'

'Thank you, Mr van der Brons, I will do that.' She got to her feet and he got up too and opened the door of the drawing-room for her. 'You are tired and I have disturbed your leisure,' she said, pausing at the door.

He denied that politely, bade her goodnight and went back to his seat by the fire. He sat there for a long time, with Samson's head on his feet, so quiet that he might have been asleep. Only he wasn't; he was thinking about Charity.

It was several days later when Charity encountered Cor as she was on her way to get the old notes of a patient who had just been admitted. The files were kept in a basement room at the back of the hospital, at the end of a passage from which led the laundry, boiler-room, stores and any number of cell-like cubby-holes used to house all the paraphernalia of a large hospital. The clerk found the notes for her while they exchanged basic English and Dutch and Charity started back on her journey to the burns unit. She was at the end of the corridor, about to run up the short staircase to the ground floor, when Cor came down it, coming to a halt in front of her, standing in her way.

'Well, well,' he cried, and grinned at her. 'If it isn't my little English friend. What is all this I hear about lunch with our good Professor van der Brons? Oh, you don't need to blush—these things get around, you know. Well, he's a better catch than I or any of us hard-working housemen. How did you manage it?' He gave a nasty little smile. 'You're a deep one, aren't you?'

Charity gave him a steady look, wondering how she could have imagined herself in love with him. 'I'm on duty—if you would move so that I can get to the stairs . . .'

'Not so fast; I'm waiting to hear how you managed to charm the most eminent professor in the hospital into inviting you to lunch. You're a sly one, I must say . . .'

Charity didn't answer, for, leaning over the stair rail at his ease, Mr van der Brons was listening to every word with interest, smiling a little. She gave him a look which was unconsciously beseeching and Cor saw it and turned round just in time to confront the professor's massive proportions.

'I suggest,' said Mr van der Brons in a gentle voice which sent a shiver down Charity's spine, 'that you make yourself scarce—van Kamp, isn't it? Apologise to the lady first and if you should at any time feel tempted to repeat this regrettable occurrence I can assure you that you will regret it.'

Charity had gone rather pale—now she went red as Cor mumbled an apology and took himself off. She drew a steadying breath and waited to hear what Mr van der Brons had to say. She felt ready to sink into the floor; hopefully he hadn't heard the whole of the conversation.

Her companion didn't choose to enlighten her. 'So fortunate that I should see you—I bear a message from Miss Bloom; she would like you to go to tea with her and the children—you're free tomorrow, are you not? About half-past two, if that suits you—the girls look forward to seeing you.'

'In the Bijenkorf?' She strove to make her voice normal, but it had a distinct wobble.

'No, no. At my house, of course. They will want to play noisy games, I dare say. Miss Bloom, bless her, is addicted to patience and old maid and an occasional fast game of snap. I believe that they are rather hoping that you will make a dolls' house...'

This prosaic conversation soothed her nerves; the ugly little incident with Cor seemed unimportant. Charity said at once, 'Oh, I'd love to, but I need boxes and things; besides, Miss Bloom might not like it. I do know some card games, though.'

'Splendid. I will tell them to expect you. Take the tram from outside the hospital gates; it stops within a hundred yards or so of the house.' He stood on one side so that she might climb the stairs. 'Tell Zuster Kingsma that I kept you.'

He went on his way, leaving her to wonder if he had heard any of the awful things Cor had said; it seemed unlikely.

Fortunately for her peace of mind, he had heard every word.

She spent the next morning washing her smalls, doing her nails and experimenting with a new lipstick, then after lunch she got into the new coat and hat and went to catch the tram. It stopped at the bridge which led to the narrow street where the professor lived, and from there it was a very short walk. She thumped the great brass knocker, feeling suddenly uncertain, to be reassured by Jolly's welcoming smile.

'I will take your coat and hat, miss.' And then, 'If you will follow me?'

She went up the staircase behind him, glad that she was wearing the needlecord dress, and was shown into a large light room where she was given a rapturous welcome by the children and a more subdued but sincere one by Miss Bloom.

The play-room, Charity saw at once, had everything in it that a child could wish for and yet at the same time it was comfortably shabby and lived-in and extremely tidy. She rather thought that Teile and Letizia might have everything to make a child happy, but had been taught to appreciate what they had. She was led round the room and shown their possessions and presently they all settled down at the table to play spillikins, an old-fashioned game which Charity hadn't played for years. The spillikins were mother-of-pearl and delicately beautiful. They inspected the dolls' house next, a magnificent mansion complete to the last teaspoon.

'You couldn't possibly want a home-made dolls' house,' cried Charity, who could have spent a happy afternoon rearranging its furniture. But it seemed that they did. She had none of the bits and pieces she would need to make one, though, so she sat down at the table and drew an exquisitely neat diagram of a modest house, two up and two down, with stairs and a bathroom and kitchen, and promised that if she should come again, which she considered unlikely once Miss Bloom had gone, she would make one. 'I would need cardboard and glue and paper,' she pointed out, 'and a box of paints...'

Miss Bloom left her sewing then and they played cards until the tea-tray was brought in: bread and butter cut thin, buns and a sponge cake. Miss Bloom, pouring out, urged Charity to make a good tea. 'For you are a little too thin, my dear,' she observed kindly. 'Perhaps when you have settled in your work...?'

Charity said that yes, she was sure to get plump if she stayed in Holland, and they all laughed just as the door opened and Mr van der Brons came in.

'Tea!' he exclaimed. 'I am not too late?' He kissed his children, patted Miss Bloom on the shoulder and kissed Charity's cheek in an absent-minded manner before sitting down in one of the roomy easychairs.

Miss Bloom rose to touch the bell. 'Fresh tea,' she said in her no-nonsense voice, 'and buns, or perhaps muffins?'

'Muffins, Miss Bloom. You have no idea how pleasant this is after the dreary afternoon outside.

'You'll stay, Papa?' asked Teile. 'Charity says she must go back soon—will you ask her to stay? We could play Scrabble...'

Jolly came in with fresh tea, the muffins and Samson, delighted to see his master. 'Do you need to go back, Charity?' asked the professor. 'I'm free for a couple of hours; if you aren't in a hurry I'll drop you off as I go past the hospital.'

Charity looked at the two small faces beaming at her. She had no reason to go back to the hospital and it was delightful in this homely room—lovely and cosy and like being one of the family. 'Thank you—then I'll stay.'

They played Scrabble, first in English and then in Dutch, and even Miss Bloom laughed at Charity's clumsy attempts to spell the Dutch words. After an hour Mr van der Brons got up. 'I'll be back,' he told them. 'Charity—I'll be twenty minutes or so—just time for a lightning game before you go.'

He was as good as his word; this time he came back in his dinner-jacket. He kissed his children good-night, told Miss Bloom to enjoy her dinner, and waited placidly while Charity made her own farewells. She made them as quickly as she could for it was obvious that Mr van der Brons had an evening engagement and wouldn't like to be kept waiting.

'Come and say goodnight when you get home, Papa?' asked Letizia.

'I shall be late, *liefje*, but I'll come and make sure that you're both asleep.'

'Where are you going, Papa?' asked Teile.

'Out to dinner and perhaps dancing, darling.'

'With Mevrouw——' Teile didn't finish what she was going to say; Miss Bloom was frowning fiercely to stop her.

Charity, ushered out of the house by an attentive Jolly, supposed that it was the same Mevrouw de Groot the children had mentioned. A widow? She speculated, sitting composedly by Mr van der Brons as he drove through the streets. She hoped that she was a nice person and that she and the children would like each other. She had the feeling that the children hadn't much of an opinion of her; perhaps they were a little jealous, naturally enough...

'I can hear you thinking,' said Mr van der Brons surprisingly. 'Turning a few crumbs of truth into a large loaf, no doubt. Don't do it, Charity—the result is always disappointing.'

'How could you possibly...?' she began, and altered it to, 'It's a bad habit I got into—oh, years ago, after my mother died. You see, if you can think you aren't lonely.' She sounded matter-of-fact. 'Anyway, I don't need to now, you know; there's the hospital and my work and the other nurses and Christmas.'

He received this muddled speech with a comfortable grunt although he said nothing, only, when they reached the hospital, leaned over and opened her door for her. 'Go straight in,' he bade her. 'Forgive me for not getting out—I'm late...'

She hopped out, uttering her thanks as she did so and topped them with a cheerful goodnight. It had been a lovely afternoon, the children were sweet and Miss Bloom, under her severe mien, was a dear. Mr van der Brons, of course, needed no praise.

Later, when she was in bed, she thought about him at some length. Cor no longer occupied her thoughts and if he did it was with amazement that she could ever have considered herself in love with him. In some way, Mr van der Brons had obliterated him from her mind, although, thinking about that, she couldn't quite discover how. He had said very little, given no tiresome advice, nor had he admonished her to be cheerful and forget the whole sorry affair, and yet he had made it possible for her to see that what she had thought was a broken heart had sustained a mere crack, already invisibly repaired. She curled up in bed with a contented sigh and went on thinking about him; he was a restful person to think about. Just before she dropped off she wondered what he was doing that evening.

He was at an old friend's house, a member of a small dinner party, apparently enjoying himself, taking part in the rather highbrow conversation, listening attentively to the remarks addressed to him by his dinner partner, a pleasant widow in her thirties—his well-meaning friends had been engaged upon the fruitless task of finding him a wife for some years—making all the right replies in an interested voice, giving her what appeared to be his full attention while he thought about Charity.

Of course he saw her on the unit during the next day or so, but only as a small gowned figure going to and fro about her work, and when she was bidden to work in Theatre he dismissed her—and everyone else for that matter—from his mind, concentrating on his meticulous work. As for Charity, she hardly expected him to do more than give his brief courteous nod when he came on to the unit each day. Indeed, she would have been surprised if he had done more; he was, she had decided, a man whose innate kindness caused him to offer help when it was needed—a lift in his car, a clean handkerchief to mop up tears, even a meal somewhere, but that didn't mean that he needed to offer friendship too. Yet he had asked her if she liked him. Perhaps she was thinking about him too much...

Christmas was almost upon them and the unit was full; none of the patients were in a fit state to go home; those with pedicles were too grotesque to leave the unit and there were several patients with severe burns, most of them children, who needed constant care. Besides, said Zuster Kingsma from experience, it was a certainty that at least one fire victim would be admitted over the Christmas period, for which reason she herself would be on duty for the two Christmas days and her staff would be on duty, taking alternate half-days. It was necessary, she pointed out, that there should be trained staff instantly available.

That was still some days away; Charity spent her two free days before then poking around the shops, buying gifts for her friends and admiring the pretty clothes in the shop windows. There would be the hospital dance in January and she was going with several of the other nurses. She had no partner, but they assured her kindly that there would be no lack of them once she was there. In the meanwhile there was the excitement of Christmas—not quite like Christmas at home, perhaps, but the shops looked magnificent and there were Christmas trees in every window.

From time to time she saw Cor but never to speak to; the moment he caught sight of her he turned about or went into a convenient door, and she, for her part, hardly noticed him.

It wanted two days to Christmas Eve when she had a note from Miss Bloom inviting her to go to tea if she were free on the following afternoon. 'I return home a few days after Christmas,' wrote Miss Bloom, 'and I am sure that you will be too busy over the Christmas period to see me. I should like to bid you goodbye.'

It so happened that Charity was free at half-past three on the following day; what was more, Zuster Kingsma allowed her to go off duty rather earlier than that, so that she had time to buy chocolates for the little girls and a pretty scarf for Miss Bloom. She got on to the tram, thankful that in Holland it was the custom to wrap presents then and there in the shop. She hugged the colourful packages to her, glad of her new coat, for the tram was half empty and cold. The icy wind struck her as she alighted at the bridge and hurried towards Mr van der Brons's house. Perhaps it was going to snow; the other nurses had talked of skating on the canals and stalls of hot chestnuts on the ice. A pity I can't skate, reflected Charity, thumping the knocker.

Jolly opened the door with a welcoming smile, took her outdoor things and led her upstairs to the play-room where Miss Bloom and the girls were waiting. She paused in the doorway, rather taken aback at the mass of paper chains and tinsel and baubles hanging from every inch of space.

'How lovely! she cried. 'Now I know it's Christmas.'

The children fell upon her and Miss Bloom said, 'I'm so glad that you could come; I dare say you won't have much free time for the next few days.'

Charity gave her presents and then sat down to admire the stack of parcels the children had wrapped up and labelled. 'We went shopping with Papa,' Teile told her. 'He gives us our pocket money and we choose what we want to buy for the presents, only we can't have any more money if we've spent it, so we have to be careful.'

'I'm sure you managed well,' said Charity, 'and I think most of us have to shop like that, so as not to overspend.'

'Papa doesn't,' said Letizia. 'He can spend all the money he likes; he's rich.'

'That will do, Letizia,' said Miss Bloom firmly. 'One doesn't discuss one's father's affairs with people.'

'He wouldn't mind me telling Charity—he likes her like he likes you, Miss Bloom.'

'Very gratifying,' said Miss Bloom, 'but all the same, his affairs are private, my dear.'

Letizia looked as though she was going to argue and Charity plunged into an account of how she had got into a muddle with her money while she was shopping and everyone laughed. Presently they gathered round the table and began a game of consequences. They played in Dutch which was hard work for Charity but added very much to the light-heartedness of the occasion.

They were having tea when Mr van der Brons walked in, to be overwhelmed by his children and

Samson. Jolly followed him in with fresh tea and more crumpets and he sat down in his chair, listening to his daughters' chatter, smiling lazily at Charity. 'I have given myself the rest of the day off,' he told them. 'Provided Charity will agree, I thought that we might all go out into the town. A look around the shops and a cup of coffee somewhere?'

He was overwhelmed once again by the little girls. 'You'll say yes, won't you, Charity? You must! Miss Bloom wants you to come, don't you, Miss Bloom?'

'Oh, indeed I do, it sounds delightful.'

So Charity said that yes, she would love to go with them, and presently they got into their outdoor things and trooped out of the house into the winter night.

Charity hadn't realised that the centre of the city was so near the house. Five minutes' walk brought them into the Heerengracht and from there it was only short distance to the Leidsestraat.

The streets were crowded with last-minute shoppers and people out to enjoy themselves. They strolled along now under the bright lights of the decorated shops, stopping to look in the windows; the professor had one small daughter at each hand and Charity and Miss Bloom followed wherever they went. Presently they had coffee in one of the big cafés on the Rembrantsplein. It was noisy and colourful and, as Mr van der Brons observed in his effortless English, 'Not quite his cup of tea,' but the little girls loved it.

They walked back presently through streets becoming even more crowded and once back in the house Charity was persuaded to have another cup of coffee before she went back to the hospital. By then it was early evening and she was anxious to be gone; probably the professor had plans of his own and she hastily invented a party in the nurses' home to which she had been invited. She uttered the fib so emphatically that he had to hide a smile but he got to his feet and declared that he was ready to drive her back, uttering the hope that the party would be fun.

She bade Miss Bloom goodbye, a final one this time, kissed the children and hugged them, and went out to the car with the faithful Samson dogging their footsteps. She didn't want to go; it had been a lovely afternoon but she had been lucky to have had it, she reminded herself briskly.

Mr van der Brons got out of the car when they reached the hospital. He opened the door for her, reiterated the hope that the party would be fun and a good one and bade her goodnight. At the last moment he bent and kissed her cold cheek. 'I shall see you tomorrow,' he told her. He smiled down into her surprised face. 'Why do you look so puzzled?'

She shook her head and blurted out, 'You kissed me—was that because it's Christmas?'

'I'll tell you tomorrow.'

He gave her a gentle shove through the door. 'Get inside; it's cold. Goodnight, Charity.'

CHAPTER FIVE

ZUSTER KINGSMA had been right; Charity went on duty the next morning to find that an old woman, sitting over an oil heater, had dozed off and fallen over, knocking the heater over at the same time. She was severely burned and frail and although Mr van der Brons, called in at four o'clock in the morning, had worked hard over her, she died. It cast a shadow over Christmas, a shadow they did their best to dispel for the sake of the other patients. Since there were no more admissions that day, nor on Christmas Eve, everyone hoped for a quiet Christmas.

Charity had had an early duty; she was free at half-past three and intended going out to have another look at the shops. Several of the nurses with whom she was friendly had gone home for Christmas and the others were on duty; to stay in the quiet sitting-room in the nurses' home seemed a dull prospect.

She went unhurriedly through the hospital on her way to her room; it was already dusk and cold in the back corridors of the hospital. She would go to a coffee house, she decided, and have coffee and a *broodje* and watch the crowds in the streets. Tomorrow she would be on duty early with Sister and in the evening she would go to Evensong at the English Church and then join the nurses who were off duty in the sitting-room and watch television.

She was met at the door of the nurses' home by Zuster Hengstma. 'You are to return if you please to the burns unit; the professor wishes to speak to you.'

Charity gulped down sudden panic. What on earth had she done or not done? She sped back the way she had come and arrived pale with fright at Sister's office.

Mr van der Brons was sitting at the desk and there was no sign of Sister. He got up when she went in, came round the desk and took her hands in his. 'Don't look like that—there is nothing wrong, but I wished to speak to you and you had gone off duty before I was free to do so.'

He was still holding her hands in a comforting grasp and some of the colour came back into her cheeks. 'I thought...' she began. 'I don't know what I thought—all the things I could have done wrong...'

'I have wanted to talk to you but there has been no opportunity; indeed I am due in Theatre in five minutes' time and this is certainly neither the time nor the place which I would have wished for. But what I have to say will take only a moment and you will have time to consider it. I have for some time considered the advantages of having a wife, Charity, someone who will love Teile and Letizia and who can understand that my work is important to me. Will you marry me, Charity?' And at her sudden gasp of surprise he said, 'Don't say anything now. Go away and think about it and we can talk about it some other time. I am aware that my proposal sounds businesslike but I see no point in wrapping it up in meaningless soft phrases; you are too sensible a girl for that. Only believe me when I say that I have a great regard for you and believe that we could be happy as a family.' He smiled suddenly and bent and kissed her. 'Now run along and think about it. I don't suppose we shall have a chance to talk again for a day or so but I will try and arrange something.'

Even if she had wanted to say anything there was no chance, for someone tapped on the door to say that they were ready for him in Theatre and, with another smile, he went away.

Charity didn't move; she was incapable of it anyway, because her head, for the moment, was empty of all thought and when her brain came alive again her reaction was one of resentment. No one had ever proposed to her before and now that she had received a proposal from a most unlikely source it had been delivered in a businesslike manner calculated to send any girl into high dudgeon. It was only after a few moments fuming that it actually struck her that Mr van der Brons had asked her to marry him. She went over all that he had said, recalling every word, and upon reflection it seemed plain to her that it had been businesslike because that was exactly what he had meant. There was no question that he was in love with her. What was it he had said?'—meaningless soft phrases'. He wanted someone to look after his little daughters now that Miss Bloom was leaving and it had to be someone who didn't expect to be the centre of his universe; the burns unit was that, or possibly Mevrouw de Groot.

One of the nurses put her head round the door, looked surprised, said, 'Sorry, I thought Sister was here,' and went away again, and Charity remembered where she was. She didn't know what was going on in Theatre, but she couldn't run the risk of meeting Mr van der Brons. She peeped out into the corridor, saw that it was empty and nipped smartly out of the unit, over to the nurses' home.

Any wish she had had to go out had been swallowed up in the wave of puzzled doubt and vexation which swept over her. She went to her room and sat there, not even thinking sensibly. It was fortunate that several of her friends among the nurses were off duty too and came knocking on her door. They were all going to the sitting-room, they told her, to sing carols; the *directrice* would be there and they would have a glass of sherry and eat *kerstkrans*, a special ring-shaped cake baked especially for Christmas, and, since she seemed incapable of sensible thought, she went with them.

She had expected to lie awake all night worrying but she slept soundly and woke with the surprising thought that everything would get sorted out without her fussing.

The unit was busy; there had been another admission during the night, a small boy who had found a box of matches. Hoofdzuster Kingsma was giving the report when Mr van der Brons came out of Theatre and came into her office. He looked grey with fatigue but he remembered to wish them all a happy Christmas before he gave her instructions about the child. 'He'll do, I think,' he finished. 'I'll be back presently to take another look.'

He had spoken in Dutch and Charity, who was beginning to get to grips with that language, wondered what sort of a Christmas Day he would have—and the little girls—Miss Bloom was still there, of course...

He didn't go at once; he had a gift for each of them and when he came to Charity he handed her a brightly wrapped packet with a smile which differed in no way from those he had given to everyone else there. She thanked him quietly before Zuster Kingsma handed over a gift from his staff. Charity had no idea what it was; she had been asked to subscribe to it but she had forgotten to ask what it was to be. It looked like a book, she thought. Wim van Beek was there too, with a bottle of sherry and chocolates. He hadn't been married long and Zuster had given him coffee-mugs from all of them. His nice face beamed round at them all. 'Ineke will be so pleased,' he assured them, and then followed Mr van der Brons out of the room.

The day's work got started, Christmas or no Christmas. The nurses snatched their coffee when they could and went to their dinners one at a time. Mr van der Brons was back during the morning and Wim van Beek also came to check on the little boy. Charity, back from a hasty meal, was sent to special the child until the nurses who were to take over came on duty.

The small boy, although horribly burned, was responding well to his treatment. Mr van der Brons had said that he would recover and Charity believed him. She was handing over to Corrie Vinke, who was to relieve her, when he came once more. Zuster Kingsma was with him and she nodded to Charity to go. She was at the door when he spoke, his back to her as he bent over his small patient. 'Zuster Pearson, Teile and Letizia wish you a happy Christmas and invite you to tea on Saturday—the twenty-eighth—may I tell them that you will come?'

He glanced briefly over his shoulder at her; his face wore its usual placid expression. No one would think... She refused to remember his proposal. On the face of it he appeared to have forgotten it too.

With a heightened colour she said in what she hoped was a matter-of-fact voice, 'Oh, how kind of them; of course I'd love to come. Please thank them.'

She escaped then, avoiding the interested glances cast in her direction.

It was at supper that evening that someone asked, 'How ever did you get to know Mr van der Brons's children, Charity?'

She had no need to answer, for several voices vied with each other to explain about the fire and how brave she had been and it was Zuster Smit who explained that Charity had been rather poorly afterwards and the professor had been kind enough to take her to his home. 'A kind of treat because Charity had burnt her hands and ruined her clothes. He is a kind man.' There was a chorus of assent and thankfully someone suggested that they should go along to the sitting-room and see what was on TV.

Charity wasn't on duty until the afternoon on the second Christmas Day, so she got up late, mooned around with some of her friends, drinking coffee and eating the biscuits which the kindly Zuster Hengstma had provided. Presently she dressed and they went down to a rather festive meal before they went on duty with the prospect of duties until ten o'clock that evening. She was to take over from Corrie again and she found that young lady itching to go. 'My boyfriend is waiting,' she confided in Charity. 'We're going dancing, and I've got a late pass; thank heaven I'm not on until tomorrow afternoon.'

Charity was bending over the small boy. 'How is he? Sister says he's going to pull through. I've had the report—the treatment hasn't changed, has it?'

'He only rouses briefly—Mr van der Brons wants him sedated for another twenty-four hours. He'll do the first dressing under anaesthetic and decide what's best then.'

Charity nodded. They had been talking in a mixture of English and Dutch for although they didn't share the same language they shared the same nursing knowledge and it was fairly easy to understand each other.

'Have fun,' said Charity.

'*Tot ziens*,' said Corrie.

Wim van Beek came presently and checked on the child's progress.

'You enjoy our Christmas?' he wanted to know.

'Oh, yes,' Charity told him, 'it's very like ours, you know. I hope you have had some time at home?'

'A few hours, and this morning I have been at home. Mr van der Brons has gone home now and I will be on duty until midnight, so please hope that there will be no emergency.'

He went away presently and she attended to her chores, wrote up her observations, drank the tea that the maid brought her during the afternoon and began on the report which Mr van der Brons would expect to have ready for him when he came in the morning.

The child was quiet; beyond the adjusting of the various appliances needed to help his recovery, and the frequent observations, there wasn't a great deal to do. The afternoon darkened and she went and switched on the shaded light by the bed. Hoofdzuster Kingsma came and went and presently it was time for her supper, and an hour later Charity, relieved by one of the other nurses, went to her own meal. Since it was Christmas the usually simple meal had been replaced by cold chicken, salad and great dishes of *pommes frites* and there was ice-cream afterwards. Nothing to drink, of course, but there was plenty of lemonade and great pots of coffee.

There were still several hours to go before she would go off duty and the next day the small excitement of Christmas would be over for another year.

She was wrong, although the admission of three teenagers who had set a room alight with smouldering cigarettes and been unable to get out of it before the whole place was afire could hardly be called a small excitement. Hoofdzuster Kingsma, after a couple of hours off duty, was there when they were admitted, and Charity could see why Mr van der Brons set such store by her; she had her off-duty staff back within ten minutes, sent the more junior nurses to take over on the wards and gathered her staff nurses to cope with the sudden influx of work. Wim van Beek and two of the housemen were there and so, within fifteen minutes, was Mr van der Brons, elegant in a dinner-jacket which he stripped off and flung down in Sister's office before being tied into a gown, listening to Wim and Sister while a nervous student nurse tied the tapes.

Charity, dealing with plasma infusions, morphia injections and the delicate task of cutting away charred clothing, didn't notice the passing of time. It was almost midnight when Sister sent her off duty and the professor was still in Theatre, the fourteen-year-old girl was back in her bed in intensive care, and the second boy was still waiting to go to Theatre.

'I'll stay if you like,' Charity offered.

'I would prefer you to come on duty at half-past seven in the morning—there will be much work,' said Hoofdzuster Kingsma. So Charity went to her bed, sleepily aware that neither Sister nor Mr van der Brons were likely to go to bed that night at all.

When she went on duty in the morning Sister had at last gone off duty and Theatre Sister had taken over. She had been there for most of the night too and after giving the report she went away, leaving the senior staff nurse to take over. There were plenty of nurses on duty and a good thing too, reflected Charity, for there was more than enough work for them all to do. Mr van der Brons and Sister came together halfway through the morning and, although his good mornings were as courteous as always, his mind was wholly on his patients. Charity, going off duty that afternoon, thought that she had never been so busy in her life before.

She had her tea, curled up on her bed and slept until suppertime, then had a shower and got into bed, blissfully aware that she wasn't working until the afternoon. It was as she was going on duty then that she remembered she was to go to tea with Teile and Letizia on the following afternoon.

The unit was back in its well-ordered routine; Mr van der Brons came and went all day with van Beek at his heels and as far as Charity was concerned she might not have been there. True, he spoke to her once or twice, but only concerning a patient, his eyes on her face, his own wearing its usual calm expression. For two pins, she thought, going off duty that evening, I won't go to tea tomorrow—a resolve swallowed up by Mr van der Brons's quiet voice the following morning.

'The children look forward to seeing you, Charity. Miss Bloom has gone and they are missing her badly.'

*   *   *

She wore the red needlecord, for it seemed right for the nice old house on the *gracht* and she wasted no time changing into it. The little girls must be feeling lonely without Miss Bloom; Charity hoped that they would have someone nice in her place. She paused, staring into the looking-glass as she brushed her hair. If—but only if—Mr van der Brons had been serious and if—and again if—she married him, there would be no need of a governess. He would be killing several birds with one stone—a governess for his little daughters, someone to act as his hostess to his friends and a listener who would understand him if he should at any time wish to discuss his work. She frowned fiercely at her own reflection. When it was put like that, she felt like rejecting the idea outright; on the other hand...

The little girls were overjoyed to see her; she was hugged and kissed while they told her about Miss Bloom. 'Papa took her to Schiphol and we gave her a present, but it's very lonely.' Teile sniffed dolefully. 'I suppose you couldn't possibly stay with us?'

'Well, I do work at the hospital, you see,' said Charity gently. 'I'm sure your father will find another governess for you.'

'We asked him and he said wait and see,' said Letizia.

'That can be quite fun sometimes,' observed Charity soothingly, and was glad to see Jolly arriving with the tea tray.

They had finished tea and were deep in the construction of a dolls' house, for, rather to Charity's surprise, the little girls had gathered together cardboard, glue, paints and paper. So after tea she spread a newspaper over the table and assembled everything she needed and began, helped and hindered by the children. She was glueing the walls together when Mr van der Brons joined them and since it was a little bit of a ticklish business she cast him only a fleeting glance, and her 'good evening' was preoccupied.

The children flung themselves at him, Samson barked joyfully, and it struck her that she might have been more friendly. She gave him rather a shy enquiring look and found him smiling at her. She was quite taken unawares when he asked, 'Well, have you thought about it, Charity?'

She glowered at him; it had been bad enough being proposed to in Sister's office and in such a down-to-earth manner too, and now she was expected to give him her answer with the two little girls, all agog, listening to every word.

He was laughing at her. 'No, no, I'm sorry, Charity, how very thoughtless of me. But you will stay this evening, won't you? Mrs Jolly is determined to excel herself. We might have dinner a little earlier, perhaps, and these two can share it.' And at their whoops of delight, he added, 'On the condition that they go to bed immediately afterwards.'

He wandered over to the table and bent over the little cardboard house, his hand on her shoulder. 'Nice,' he observed. 'I won't disturb you for a while— I've some work to do. I'll be back.' He went away, taking Samson with him, and Charity was very surprised to find that she missed him.

They dined presently; a treat for the children because they were still sad at Miss Bloom's going and Mrs Jolly had indeed excelled herself—mushrooms in garlic, *poulet a l'estragon* served with creamed potatoes and pumpkin soufflé, followed by a coffee

Bavarois. The little girls had been allowed a thimble-ful of wine; a white wine which Charity pronounced delicious and enquired in her sensible way as to its name.

The professor hid a gentle amusement but answered her gravely. 'It is a white burgundy, rather dry for your taste perhaps?'

'I think it is just right, but of course I don't know much about wine.'

She applied herself to her chicken with an unself-conscious appetite, something which he found very refreshing after the jaded palates of the women he had occasionally asked out to dinner. Miss Bloom had described her as a nice girl and she was; he liked her very much, and she would fit into their lives very well, slipping into their way of living without disturbing it in any way. He smiled warmly at her across the table and she smiled back at him, thinking that when he was there her small worries and anxieties seemed to disappear.

The little girls went to bed, led away by a plump smiling girl whom Mr van der Brons introduced as Nel. 'She is what you call a housemaid, I think; she is also very good with the children when Miss Bloom is not here.'

He paused and took the coffee-cup she was of-fering. They were in the drawing-room now, sitting one each side of the brisk fire with Samson between them. 'Charity, I very much hope that you are going to tell me that you will marry me. I am a little out of practice with pretty speeches. I can but reiterate what I have already told you: that I think that we could build a happy home-life for the children together. To say more—to promise more—would be wrong, but unlike young van Kamp I do mean what I say.'

Charity sat very still; she had gone rather pale but she looked at him calmly. She believed him, but before she could answer him there were one or two points to settle. 'If I marry you you will believe me when I say that although it will be very nice to live here in comfort and have the children to love and look after and have pretty clothes, I dare say, I wouldn't be doing it for any of those things. I'm fond of Teile and Letizia, and if you were a struggling GP I'd be just as willing to marry you. I—I like you and I think we could be content together. Only I don't love you, you know...' She paused. 'I'm making a muddle of it, but do you understand?'

He was smiling a little. 'Oh, yes, and I think we might leave the romantic side of it for the time being, don't you? Neither of us is impulsive and both of us have tried romance and found it—what shall I say?— disappointing. A calm friendship will suit us both, will it not?'

Charity drew a deep breath. 'Well, then, I'll marry you if you really want me to.'

He got out of his chair and came to pluck her gently from hers. His hands on her shoulders were gentle and his voice was gentle too.

'I believe that we shall deal together very well...' he bent and kissed her cheek '...and the children will be enchanted.'

'You're sure? I'm not at all like Miss Bloom.'

He laughed then. 'No, not in the slightest. Shall we marry soon? And do you wish to be married in England or here—there is the English Church in the

Begijnhof, just off the Kalverstraat, I expect you know of it? We can marry there.'

'I would like that. But don't I have to fulfil my contract—I can't just leave?'

'Leave that to me. Have you friends in England whom you would like to come to our wedding? I know that you have a stepsister...'

'I've friends there, yes—nurses mostly. It's well— it's rather expensive and a long way for them to come just for our wedding and I don't suppose they could afford it. I don't know where Eunice is. I had a card at Christmas but it was posted in Zurich. I've got her London address, though.'

'Then shall we have a very quiet wedding? Just you and me, someone to give you away and someone else to be best man? The children, of course... I'll take you to meet my family afterwards—I can manage a few days off at the end of January.'

She thought about it and then said matter-of-factly, 'That seems a good idea. You wouldn't mind? I mean, not having a proper wedding? Your family won't mind either?'

His mouth twitched. 'No, but they will be delighted to welcome you. Just leave everything to me, will you, my dear? I'll see about a licence—perhaps in a week's time?'

'A week?' Her voice came out in a squeak. 'But I must do some shopping.'

'Just something for the wedding. You can shop all you want to afterwards. You have the early shift tomorrow, haven't you? Come here to tea, I'll come home as soon as I can. I shall tell the children at breakfast.'

It all sounded so simple; she could leave everything to him and she was quite sure that it would be exactly as he had said. 'Supposing it doesn't work out?' She sounded anxious.

'But it will.' *He* sounded quite certain and she felt reassured.

'It's for the rest of our lives,' she reminded him.

'Indeed it is. That is why we have a good chance of making a success of it. We have good reasons to marry, Charity, not sudden whims or infatuation—we both know about those, do we not?'

It was on the tip of her tongue to ask about Mevrouw de Groot, but she stopped in time. Probably she was an old family friend and really she didn't know Mr van der Brons well enough to ask. It occurred to her then that she didn't know his name.

'Tyco—and forty years old next birthday. Too old for you, Charity?'

She shook her head. 'I hadn't thought about it, but no, I don't think it will matter at all.'

He said slowly, 'When I'm seventy you will be a sprightly fifty-three.'

'Well, if you are feeling your age, which I very much doubt, I'll be young enough to look after you, won't I?' She spoke in such a matter-of-fact way that he burst out laughing.

'I find myself looking forward to a delightful old age.' He took her hands in his and she smiled up at him.

'I should go back, please; it's quite late and I'm on duty early.'

He drove her back to the hospital with a promptitude which pleased her at first but later on gave rise to the niggling doubt that he had had enough of her company now that he had got what he wanted. She wondered, as she lay in bed, waiting for sleep, just what the future held for her and if she had been wise to agree so quickly to his proposal, and yet, although she couldn't put a finger on it, she felt that her reasons for doing so had been right. She was too sleepy to remember them anyway.

Mr van der Brons arrived at an early hour the next morning but, after examining the worst of his patients, went away, to return again this time with Wim van Beek, who started on the ward round with the most senior staff nurse while Mr van der Brons went into Sister's office. Charity was in one of the side-wards feeding the small boy who had been playing with matches. He was a cheerful child despite his burnt hands and in a few days he would be moved in with the other convalescent children. Now he sat propped up in his little bed, chattering away to her, not caring that she understood perhaps one word in ten; their conversation, conducted in two languages, one of which was unintelligible to each of them, was quite satisfactory to them both; they laughed a lot while she spooned porridge into his eager little mouth and then patiently held bread and butter and cheese for him to gobble. They were giggling together when Sister and Mr van der Brons came in.

'So we are to lose you,' said Hoofdzuster Kingsma cheerfully. 'It is a great surprise to us, but we are also pleased for you both and wish you every happiness.'

Charity fed her patient another finger of bread and cheese and looked reproachfully at Mr van der Brons—a look he ignored with blandness.

'Oh, well,' observed Charity, at a loss for words until he observed genially,

'The *directrice* and Sister Kingsma are kind enough to allow you to leave at the end of the week, Charity. We are most grateful, are we not?'

She caught his eye and decided that he was amused about the whole thing. 'Most grateful,' she repeated, wondering where she was to go until he had made arrangements for the wedding. Presumably he would let her know when he saw fit. She gave him another look, questioning and rather cross, and he said,

'We'll discuss the details this evening.'

He became all at once brisk. 'We might take a look at this little chap—a skin graft on the left hand, I think. As soon as possible we will send him home and then have him back to see what can be done. His mother is a very sensible woman and once we can have these bandages off she should be able to look after him.' He turned to Zuster Kingsma. 'There are no other children?' He switched to Dutch and Charity finished feeding the bread and cheese and offered milk through a straw. She was feeling annoyed; Mr van der Brons was arranging everything to suit himself. She had always thought herself that the bride made all the decisions, but here he was, making plans without so much as a by-your-leave...

She stayed cross all day and went off duty that afternoon in something of a bad temper. She had been overwhelmed by the good wishes of her friends when she went to her dinner; the grapevine was as strong in Holland as it was in England, apparently, although she hadn't said a word to anyone, and to their excited questions as to when she was to marry and where she was to live and when she was going to leave she had to give vague answers, being not much wiser than they were.

However, it was impossible to stay cross when she reached Mr van der Brons's house; the little girls fell upon her and there was no doubt that they were happy at the news. 'What shall we call you?' they wanted to know, and, what was more important, 'What are you going to wear at the wedding?'

Charity's peevishness melted before their delight. 'Well, I haven't had time to think about it. Have you any ideas?'

They were bursting with them. Their shrill voices rang with suggestions; white satin, yards of lace, pearl-embroidered veils, satin slippers, long white gloves...!

'Well,' said Charity cautiously, 'I rather thought as it is to be a very quiet wedding that I might wear a dress and jacket.' At the look of disappointment on their faces, she added hastily, 'Silk, of course, and in a pretty colour and a hat. I couldn't wear satin slippers but I could have, well—patent leather? You know, shiny and black?'

They were having tea and arguing happily about what should go on the hat when Mr van der Brons joined them. His daughters hurled themselves at him with Samson weaving in and out.

'Charity wants to wear a hat,' they told him. 'She doesn't want to look like a proper bride.' They lapsed into Dutch and he listened patiently.

'Of course she will look like a bride,' he assured them. 'I rather fancy a hat myself and a large bouquet...very bridal.'

He came across to where Charity was sitting and bent to kiss her cheek. 'I am sure that you will be a charming bride,' he told her kindly. 'Now, supposing we take Charity round her new home.'

They set off, the four of them and Samson, of course. The drawing-room she had already seen but she was taken on a tour of the family portraits on its walls and then led across the hall to the dining-room where there were even more portraits. 'I'm afraid our family is a vast one, and the ancestor who built this house had ten children who astonishingly all survived to enlarge the family even more.'

There was a smaller room behind the dining-room, a sitting-room, very cosy and charmingly furnished, and, on the other side of the hall, the study. She peeped inside to admire the vast desk, rows of book-shelves and the comfortable leather armchairs on each side of the old fashioned stove.

Upstairs she was led in and out of any number of bedrooms; from the street the house hadn't appeared all that vast, but inside it was a rabbit warren of rooms and small passages. They mounted even higher to find still more bedrooms and then up a staircase there was the flat where the Jollys lived.

'There's a cellar too,' Mr van der Brons told her, 'but we'll leave that for another time.'

They all went down to the drawing-room again and presently the little girls went with Nel to have their supper. 'They will be back to say goodnight,' said Mr van der Brons, 'but I suspect that when you come to live with us you will be expected to tuck them up at bedtime. A task I have undertaken when I have been at home, for Miss Bloom, bless her, didn't hold with cuddles and kisses although she was always kind to the children.'

He invited her to sit in a chair by the fire and fetched their drinks from the rent table which stood between the windows. 'Now let us get things clear. You are to leave at the end of next week—Saturday. I have arranged a special licence and we can be married that afternoon and come back here. I have arranged to be free on the Sunday but I have a list on the Monday morning. Perhaps we can take a holiday later on. I have a croft in Scotland—in the Highlands—and a small villa in Portugal; we could go to whichever one you would like.'

'What about the children?'

'They might come with us.' He spoke casually. 'They'll be going to school next week and I suppose we could wait until the Easter holidays.'

She agreed quietly, conscious of disappointment— to get to know each other would be nice, she thought wistfully and then told herself bracingly that it was early days; they weren't even married yet. She wasn't even quite sure if they were engaged. A doubt which was set at rest within the next few minutes, for he opened a drawer in the rent table and took out a small velvet box.

'My grandmother gave me this a long time ago and told me to give it to whoever I married. My first wife wanted a modern ring but I think that it will be right for you, Charity.'

The ring was a sapphire set in diamonds, old-fashioned but beautiful. What was more it fitted her finger.

'It's beautiful, and thank you very much.' She added softly, 'I hope your granny would have liked me.'

'I am quite sure of it. Now let us get down to details.' He had it all planned, all she had to do was to buy herself whatever clothes she needed. 'One other thing—have you enough money?'

'Yes, oh, yes, thank you.'

He nodded carelessly. 'You will of course get all the clothes you want when we are married. Later on I will discuss ways and means with you; in the meantime, spend what you wish.'

She thanked him, thinking all the while that it was a good thing she wasn't Eunice, who would have taken him at his word and bought up half the boutiques in the city.

They had their dinner presently after the children had come downstairs to say goodnight and their wedding wasn't mentioned again, only when she got up to go away back to the hospital he said casually, 'The girls will want new dresses for the wedding—will you see to that? Take them to La Bonneterie, will you, and let them choose within reason? It has always seemed to me that Miss Bloom dressed them rather soberly—I've an account there, so please get what they need and charge it.'

He drove her back and saw her into the hospital before going in search of Wim van Beek, who was still on duty. His goodnight was cheerful and brisk. He wore the air of a man who had arranged things to suit himself and was pleased with the result. She had no doubt that once she was out of sight he would have forgotten her. She might be making the mistake of a lifetime, and yet some deep feeling urged her to accept the future.

CHAPTER SIX

CHARITY'S engagement caused something of a stir in the hospital. Her friends among the nurses were frankly envious but not unkindly so, for she was well liked and, although Cor van Kamp would have ridiculed the whole thing if he had had the chance, the snide remarks he let fall were received with amused contempt, for Mr van der Brons was popular too and respected throughout the hospital. There was a whip-round for a wedding present and plans for those who could to attend the wedding. However, the plans came to nothing since no one was able to discover just when it was to take place. Mr van der Brons, although respected and liked, was nevertheless known to keep his private life private; not even Wim van Beek could summon the courage to ask him outright about the wedding. Mr van der Brons was of course aware of this, going on in his placid way, accepting congratulations with a bland smile which somehow prevented anyone's asking questions.

As for Charity, she smiled and suggested that Mr van der Brons would tell them.

There was almost a week before the wedding and on the days when she was off duty in the afternoon she went along to the house on the *gracht* to have discussions with the children about the arrangements and what exactly they wanted to wear. For ten-year-olds they had very definite ideas. Miss Bloom had never allowed them to choose their clothes and now

Charity had to persuade them not to decide upon anything too outrageous. She spent some time with the children at La Bonneterie and, by dint of cunning and diplomacy, persuaded them into sapphire-blue velvet dresses, matching fine wool jackets and velvet berets. She considered the price astronomical but their father had said buy what they wanted... As for herself, she combed the shops for an outfit which would suit both her person and her pocket. Her first choice—a suit in some sort of silky material—didn't seem practical; the weather had turned very cold with occasional flurries of snow, and she was wise enough to know that her nondescript looks would suffer if she shivered throughout the ceremony. It was almost lunchtime and she was feeling desperate and peevish when she saw what would do very nicely in one of the small smart boutiques in P.C. Hoofstraat. A suit in fine wool, a shade darker than the children's outfits, beautifully cut and with a matching blouse in oyster crêpe de Chine.

It was far more money than she had intended to pay but standing in front of the mirror, studying her person, she saw that it did something for her. The saleslady nodded approval and mentioned in excellent English that she just so happened to have the very hat to go with it.

She was quite right, it was a dear little hat, adding elegance to Charity's mildly brown locks, and she handed over a sizeable wadge of notes without a qualm. She was almost penniless by the time she got back to the hospital, but she had added patent-leather pumps, a matching handbag and black kid gloves, soft as silk and the reason for her having only a few *gulden* in her purse.

She went to the professor's house one evening soon after to spend some time with the little girls and then, when they had gone to bed, to dine with Tyco.

They had slipped into a pleasant relationship; they found enough to talk about for they were interested in the same things, although Charity regretted that Tyco made no effort at serious conversation. She knew very little about him; in fact, she wasn't sure that she had even glimpsed the real Tyco behind his placid manner but somehow when she had from time to time plucked up courage to ask him about his life, he had blandly avoided an answer. Perhaps when she met his family she would learn more. Common sense told her that it was madness to marry a man she hardly knew— that wasn't quite true, of course; she knew him for a kind man, generous and patient, much liked by his patients and the hospital staff. He was a good father too and she felt in her bones, despite occasional doubts in the small hours, that he would be a good husband. That he liked her she was sure but she wasn't the be-all and end-all of his life. She supposed that years ago they would have called it a marriage of convenience.

He made no attempt to keep her when she suggested that she should go back to the hospital, but drove her back, saw her as far as the nurses' home and reminded her that he was operating in den Haag in the morning. 'I dare say I shan't see you tomorrow,' he said, 'but do go home if you like. Jolly will bring you back. I shall be very late home.'

'I've a few things I need to do,' said Charity rather too quickly, 'but if I may I'll see Teile and Letizia on Friday morning and make sure their dresses are quite all right. A kind of dress rehearsal...'

'Do that. I dare say we'll see each other on Friday.' He bent and kissed her cheek. 'Goodnight, Charity.'

On Friday morning, since she was off duty until three o'clock, she went to see the children and spent a happy hour or so helping them to try on their new clothes, and since there was no sign of Tyco she left just before lunch with the plea that she still had to pack her things. Which wasn't true; she had already done that but if he came home and found her there she thought he might feel that she should be invited to stay for lunch.

On duty again presently she was told that he had gone to Leiden to do a skin graft on a patient who had been sent there from Amsterdam. There was no sign of him for the rest of the day and she went off duty that evening feeling uncertain and worried about everything. She had bidden everyone on the unit goodbye, listened composedly to a good deal of teasing from her friends at supper that evening, and now she went to her bed, her cases packed and ready to be sent to her new home, her wedding outfit hanging in the wardrobe. It was a bit late in the day, she thought desperately, but there was still time to change her mind. She must have been mad to have agreed to marry Tyco; supposing his family didn't like her? Supposing he were to fall in love with another woman? Someone who would take on the role of his wife with more success than she could hope to? She got into bed, still worrying, and was still lying awake when Zuster Hengstma tapped on her door and summoned her to the telephone. 'I said you were in bed, but they wouldn't take no for an answer.'

Who was 'they'? asked Charity to herself, nipping smartly downstairs. Eunice? Her stepmother? Miss

Bloom, her mother miraculously restored to health and on her way back—in which case she herself would not be needed, would she?

She picked up the receiver and said 'Yes?' in a sharp voice which covered disquiet.

'I have got you out of bed,' said Mr van der Brons, and he sounded as though he were laughing, 'but I want you to have a good night's sleep and I am willing to wager a month's fees that you are tossing and turning and trying to make up your mind whether to creep away during the night or write me a polite note saying that you had had second thoughts.'

Charity, suddenly feeling light as a feather, beamed on the telephone. 'How ever did you know? And you are quite right—I was just being silly.'

'Now go to bed again and sleep, Charity, and mind you're quite ready in the morning.'

He rang off before she could say goodnight. He might at least have waited until she had done so. She would have felt better about it had she known that he was on his way to scrub for an emergency which had just been admitted. As for Mr van der Brons, although he had made time to ring her, guessing that she might be feeling uncertain at the last moment, his powerful brain was almost wholly concerned with the patient on the operating table.

Charity slept soundly, rose betimes and was ready and waiting when Zuster Hengstma came to fetch her. Her cases had already gone; now she went down to the entrance where Professor ter Appel was waiting to drive her to the church and give her away. There was a small crowd waiting for her; friends among the nurses, Hoofdzuster Kingsma and even the *directrice*, all wishing to express their hopes for her happy future.

She turned to look at them all as Professor ter Appel shot away from the entrance, conscious that she was leaving the known for the unknown and not very sure about it despite Tyco's words. Perhaps it was fortunate that the professor was a bad and ill-tempered driver, for she was kept fully occupied in maintaining calm as he hurtled between trams, overtook other cars, frequently shaking his fist at the drivers and whipping through traffic lights with seconds to spare, all the while keeping up a muttered monologue. Yet the moment he stopped outside the church and got out of the car to help her out he was once more an affable middle-aged man, beaming at her in a fatherly fashion and telling her not to be nervous.

There was an old man in the church porch, the verger, she supposed, who handed her a pretty little bouquet—lily-of-the-valley, pink roses, orange blossom and blue hyacinths—and wished her well before pushing open the inner door of the little church.

Tyco had promised her a quiet wedding and he had kept his word. Wim van Beek was there as his best man, his wife, the Jollys and Teile and Letizia and, edging past Charity as she stood beside the professor in the doorway, the *directrice*, Hoofdzuster Kingsma and Zuster Hengstma, who slid into their seats as she started down the aisle.

Tyco turned round and smiled at her and she smiled back, suddenly quite sure that everything was going to be all right. She smiled at the children too and then took her place beside Tyco, listening to the rector's quiet voice without hearing the words. She looked at the ring on her finger and then up at Tyco and he gave her hand a gentle squeeze and smiled very faintly. She signed the register with a steady hand and then stood beside him while Wim and Jolly took photos and everyone told her how pretty she looked and what a delightful wedding it had been.

She had no idea what was to happen next until Tyco said cheerfully, 'Well, shall we all gather at the house? Charity and the children come with me and we can squeeze in the rector. Wim, will you take the *directrice*? And Nel and Zuster Hengstma can go with Professor ter Appel.'

The Jollys had already driven away and when they all reached the house, Jolly was there at the door to admit them.

Somebody, she didn't know who, had taken a great deal of trouble. The drawing-room welcomed them with a blazing fire, charming arrangements of flowers and a table laden with drinks and canapés. Once they were all assembled Jolly came in with champagne in an ice bucket and there was the pleasant ritual of toasting the bride and groom. Charity, who had been too excited to eat any breakfast, felt the champagne whizz round her head and ate one of canapés which Nel was handing round in the doubtful hope that it might mop up the wine. By the time Jolly appeared to say that lunch was ready everyone was in the best of spirits and trooped across the hall to sit around the table, their tongues nicely loosened by the champagne.

Charity, led to the foot of the table opposite Tyco, had the feeling that she shouldn't be there, but Professor ter Appel on one side of her and Wim on the other kept up a steady flow of conversation so that she had no chance to feel awkward, and the sight of Tyco, sitting at the head of the table, looking for all the world as though he got married every day of the week, steadied her. The food dispelled the light-headed feeling that she had had; lobster mousse, with a champagne sauce, *noisettes* of lamb with a garlic-flavoured sauce and biscuit *glace* with fresh raspberries and as a finale more champagne and a wedding-cake borne in by Jolly, who was followed by the household staff. Charity and Tyco cut it together amid a good deal of hand-clapping and cheerful chatter before Jolly sliced it neatly and it was handed round to everyone there. It was nice, thought Charity, to see what she supposed to be the gardener tucking into a large slice and drinking down his champagne with gusto. Everyone went back to the drawing-room after that for coffee and more talk, and, sitting beside Tyco, she began to enjoy herself. She didn't feel married but she felt very content; his placid good nature had the effect of soothing her and the children's delight at having her in the family gave her a pleasant feeling of being wanted, of belonging.

Presently Jolly brought in the tea-tray and shortly afterwards the guests started to leave. As Wim and his wife, the last to go, went through the door, Charity said, 'What a lovely wedding; thank you very much, Tyco!'

At his casual, 'I'm glad you enjoyed it, my dear,' she felt reassuringly warmed, so it was all the more disappointing when he told her that he would have to go back to the hospital that evening. 'However, I should be back for dinner—I'll phone if I'm held up and perhaps you will ask Mrs Jolly to keep everything hot. Before I go, have you seen your room yet? I should have thought of that earlier. Teile and Letizia will show it to you, won't you, *liefjes*? And bed at the usual time, please; it has been an exciting day.'

Looking at his calm face, Charity thought it unlikely that he had been excited; satisfied perhaps, that everything had gone according to his plans, but she had no illusions about herself. There was nothing about her to excite him—that was why he had chosen her. There was no chance of her disturbing the life he had organised so successfully. He had never pretended to be anything but a friend, marrying her for the sake of the small girls, sure that they would get on well together. She had wondered at his choice of her but now she thought she knew why. She said cheerfully, 'It was a delightful party and they both looked very pretty, didn't they? I'll see that they're in bed at the usual time but I'm hoping they'll help me to unpack before they have their supper.'

'Oh, good. I'll be up to see you when I get home,' he promised the children and bent to kiss them and then kissed Charity's cheek too.

Her room was charming and blissfully comfortable. The children opened drawers, inspected the enormous clothes cupboard along one wall, took her on to the balcony outside the french windows so that she could admire the surprisingly long garden beneath them, and then took her on a tour of the bathroom, white and pearly pink and housing every conceivable aid to beautifying one's person. Then they helped her unpack, remarking with the candour of youth that she didn't seem to have many clothes. 'Never mind,' said Letizia kindly, 'Papa will buy you all the things you want to have.'

She eyed Charity's scant wardrobe, laid out tidily on the pastel pinks and blues of the bedspread. 'I suppose you didn't go to parties a great deal?'

'Well, no. I never had much time, you know; it's quite a long day at the hospital.'

'We'll come shopping with you and tell you what you must buy,' said Teile. 'Papa will pay.'

They had their supper and long-drawn-out baths, but she had them tucked up in bed presently, kissed them goodnight and went back to her room to do her face and hair rather anxiously. Perhaps it would be a good thing if she were to have a perm and go somewhere to have a professional make-up. Rather disheartened by the ordinary face which stared back at her from the looking glass on the tulipwood dressing-table, she went downstairs to find Tyco sitting in his chair, reading the paper.

He got up as she went in. 'I'm just back and hopefully I shan't need to go in until Monday.' He came to her and took her hands in his. 'I cannot begin to tell you how sorry I am that I had to leave you on our wedding-day...'

'An emergency? Of course you had to go.'

He smiled down at her. 'I can see that you will be an exemplary wife. Yes, one of the teenagers—remember? We had to have him back in theatre, but just now I think he'll do. Wim is on duty and he'll let me know if things go wrong again, but I don't think they will.'

He sat down opposite her and Jolly came in beaming.

'Champagne cocktails,' said Tyco and, when Jolly had gone, 'How pleasant it is to sit here with my wife; you are a very restful person, Charity.'

She sipped her drink. 'Oh, am I? I have very little conversation, you know.'

He smiled a little. 'To come home to someone who isn't going to chatter and is willing to listen to me while I ponder the day's work is any man's dream. Were the children good?'

'Delightful. They are dears.'

'I think so too. Next week, if you wish, you must all go shopping—I'll open an account for you at La Bonneterie and de Bijankorf and arrange for you to have a cheque-book. We had better go to the bank together—perhaps on Monday—I'm not operating until two o'clock and the round should be over by midday.'

Jolly came to tell them that dinner was served and they sat down at the table, this time with her beside him, so that they could go on talking while they ate the delicious dinner which Mrs Jolly had cooked. Afterwards in the drawing-room, while they had their coffee, he observed, 'I think that we will spend the day with my family tomorrow.'

Charity put the delicate porcelain cup carefully into its saucer. 'Here in Amsterdam?'

'No. In the north, Friesland—I am from Friesland; my family have lived there for a long time. They will all be there to meet you and make you welcome, all save Lucia in Edinburgh. When I can snatch a weekend we will go and see her too.'

'I—I hope your family will like me, I mean it must be a bit sudden for them to have . . . that is, did they know that you were going to marry me?'

'Indeed they did, and approved it.' He gave her a placid smile. 'You looked charming today; wear that blue thing tomorrow so that they can see how you looked as a bride.'

She seized on what mattered most. 'You like it? I'm glad, but I don't need to wear the hat, do I?'

The twinkle in his eyes belied his calm, 'Oh, no—we shall be in the car all the time—take a scarf or something to tie round your head if we should go out of doors. It is rather more north than Amsterdam, and colder.'

She longed to ask him about his family and his home, but she couldn't think how to start, which was a good thing for he had no more to say about it but began to talk about the children.

'They are happy at school and will be even happier now that they have you to come home to, but don't feel that you must spend all your days with them; Mrs Jolly and Nel are both reliable and devoted. It would be nice though if you would get them fitted out with some pretty dresses and so on. Miss Bloom was an excellent woman but her ideas about small girls' clothes were a little old-fashioned. They looked very nice today; one or two pretty dresses might not come amiss. Get whatever you want for yourself. Now that I have a wife we must entertain a little and we shall get asked out from time to time. We will go into finances when we are at the bank.'

'Thank you, Tyco. I haven't many clothes and I don't think they're quite suitable for a—a consultant's wife.'

'Well, go ahead with your shopping. The children go back to school in two days' time; they come home for lunch from noon until one o'clock.'

'Do I take them to school and fetch them?'

'If you can do so without disturbing your day—Nel can always take them or fetch them if you are busy.'

'I'd like to go with them.'

'They will like that; the other children have mothers and that is something they have missed.'

They talked comfortably about nothing much after that and presently Charity said that she would go to bed, a little chagrined at the smartness with which he rose from his chair to open the door. She must remember not to take up too much of his time; start some knitting or embroidery so that if he wanted to read he could do so without feeling that he should talk to her. She said goodnight in her quiet voice and he put a large hand on her shoulder. 'Goodnight, Charity. We are going to be happy together, you know.'

She wished she felt as certain of that as he had sounded.

They set off directly after breakfast the next morning, the little girls in the back with Samson, all three of them in the best of spirits and Charity sitting beside Tyco.

It was a fast drive for most of the way, he had told her, for once they were free of Amsterdam's outskirts there was the *autosnelweg*—the motorway—as far as the *Afsluitdijk*. It was a mere twelve miles to Leeuwarden from there and half an hour's drive south of the city to his home.

They stopped at a hotel for coffee a few miles before they reached the *Afsluitdijk* and then raced along it, the enclosed Ijsselmeer on one side, grey and cold under a winter sky, and the high sea dike on the other side shutting out the Waddenzee. They were almost across before she saw Friesland looming up in the distance and then they were on land again, with the signposts written in Fries as well as Dutch.

Tyco slowed through a small town. 'Harlingen,' he told her briefly and then, after a few more miles, 'Franeker—a lovely little town—we'll show it to you one day.'

Then they were weaving their way through Leeuwarden and out of it again, going south now into the country. Flat wide fields, narrow canals, farms with huge barns at their backs and presently a glimpse of grey water.

They were on a narrow road now and there had been no village for some miles but presently she saw a church ahead of them with a ring of red-roofed houses around it and leafless trees beyond. 'Rengerwoude,' said Tyco, and she heard the warmth in his voice.

'We're here,' shouted the children, 'we're almost here, look, Charity, do look...'

She looked, seeing the road ahead sweep round the church and away again and now there was a high wall on one side of the road and then a wide gateway, its wrought-iron gates thrown back. She hadn't known what to expect, certainly not the large square house at the end of the drive with its pointed roof and orderly row of windows overlooking what seemed to her to be more of a small park than a garden.

Tyco drew up before a flight of steps leading to a massive door. 'You may get out, *liefjes*, but carefully.' He got out too, saw them safely on to the raked gravel, and opened Charity's door, Samson at his heels.

'Welcome to our home, my dear.' He took her hand and they all crossed the drive and started up the steps. The door was thrown open before they reached it by an old man, white-haired but erect, who shook Tyco's hand, submitted to hugs from the little girls and, introduced as Bas, shook Charity's hand. His, *'Welkom, mevrouw,'* took her by surprise; she hadn't got used to the idea of being *mevrouw*, but it was warm and his smile was fatherly. She took heart from it as they followed the children into the square hall to be immediately engulfed by a wave of people who surged from double doors to one side.

Tyco had her hand fast in his and she found herself facing an elderly man who could only be his father and a short plump lady with bright blue eyes in a plain face. The face was kind and wore a beaming smile and Charity smiled back widely, aware of relief; she had steeled herself to meet a majestic Dutch matron who would look at her as though she were not good enough for her son and here was a dear little lady, kissing her cheek and speaking in English as good as her own.

'My dear, welcome to the family—such a lot of us, I'm afraid, but all so anxious to meet you. You didn't mind that we were not at your wedding? Tyco wanted it to be very quiet—just the ceremony, you know, but now we shall celebrate, all of us together.'

She handed her over to Tyco's father and Tyco kissed his mother and then became surrounded by his family. His father was as nice as his mother, thought Charity, an elderly version of his son, and suddenly she felt happy to be one of such a large family.

They swarmed round her now, Reka and Fenna, tall good-looking young women, and Illand and Loek, a good deal younger than Tyco and almost as large, shaking her hand, kissing her, saying how glad they were to meet her, and all the while Letizia and Teile

were darting round as well as Samson and two labra-
dors. She felt her arm gently taken.

'Reka is thirty-four,' said Tyco half laughing. 'She
is married; her husband will come presently with her
children—two, a boy and a girl. They live in
Leeuwarden. Fenna is twenty-four, engaged to a naval
officer at sea. Lucia is twenty-one—you know of her.
Illand is thirty-six, married with four children, and
his wife with them will join us for lunch. Loek is
twenty-eight and a bachelor; he is at Leiden—a doctor
too. Illand lives in Bolsward, and he is a solicitor; no
one will mind if you get them mixed up.'

She was passed from one to the other, drinking
coffee and biting at little buttery biscuits until she was
borne away with the children to take off her jacket
and tidy herself.

The house was very large; vast doors opened from
the hall and at the head of a massive staircase there
were passages leading in all directions from the gallery.
She was led to a bedroom furnished with mahogany
and very beautiful brocade where she sat down before
the triple looking-glass and did her face and tidied
her already tidy hair under the friendly eyes of her
new sisters-in-law, the children and a very old lady
whom everyone called Nanny. Charity was introduced to her and looked over by two beady black eyes.
Nanny nodded her head in a satisfactory way. 'You'll
do very well,' she told an astonished Charity. 'No
looks to speak of—but that says nothing—but nice
kind eyes and a soft mouth.'

At Charity's look of enquiry Reka said, 'Oh, good,
Nanny likes you. She's been with us for ever—nursed
Tyco, if you can believe that. Never liked his first

wife—nor did we.' She had spoken softly so that only Charity heard her.

'Oh, I do hope that I'll do,' answered Charity fervently.

They lunched in splendour in a large dining-room at a table seating a score of persons comfortably. The little mushroom pancakes, roast duckling with cherry sauce, a variety of vegetables, followed by a chocolate pudding which melted in the mouth, was every bit as good as the meals Mrs Jolly presented. Charity, sitting by Tyco, contrived to glance around her during the meal. The furniture was heavy and dark and massive and the walls above the panelling almost concealed by heavily framed paintings. There was an enormous chandelier above their heads and a thick carpet on the polished floor. She reflected that if she had had even an inkling of the lifestyle Tyco enjoyed she would have thought twice about marrying him. Then she would never have seen him again nor his delightful children and equally delightful family. He put a hand over hers as it lay on the table and turned to smile at her and she thought in a muddled way that she would have married him whatever he was.

They all went walking in the park around the house after lunch, well wrapped up against the cold wind, Mevrouw van der Brons in a voluminous cloak and Charity bundled into a hooded coat several sizes too large for her, and when they got back indoors it was to find tea waiting for them round the roaring fire in the drawing-room and once again Charity was passed from one to the other, getting to know Reka's husband and children and Illand's wife and family. She supposed that in time she would be able to tell them all apart.

They left after tea, for the weather was worsening and it was already a deep dusk. Everyone crowded into the hall to say goodbye and when Tyco's mother kissed her she pressed a small box into her hand. 'A wedding present to my new daughter,' she said and kissed her again. 'You will be happy together and the children love you.'

Mrs Jolly, on her mettle, presented them with a delicious dinner when they got home and the four of them had it together before Charity, mindful of her new status, saw the two little girls off to bed, tucked them up and went downstairs to tell Tyco that they were waiting to say goodnight to him. He wasn't in the drawing-room; she peeped into the dining-room, the small sitting-room, and then tapped on the study door and went in. He was on the phone and looked up frowning as she went in so that she said hesitantly, 'I don't mean to disturb you, but Letizia and Teile are waiting for you to say goodnight.'

He held the phone in his hand. 'I'll be up in a minute,' he said, wanting her to go away so obviously that she went without a word.

There were books in the small sitting-room; she wandered in there and chose one, taking her time, feeling uncertain. Presently he found her there. 'Come into the drawing-room for an hour?' he asked her. 'We have seen very little of each other all day; it will be pleasant to talk quietly.'

It was indeed pleasant to mull over the day, sitting opposite him with Samson at his feet and Mrs Jolly's elderly cat Crispin curled up on her lap. Yet she still went to bed presently none the wiser about the man she had married. He had been kind and courteous, putting her at her ease while at the same time telling her nothing of himself.

Patience, she told herself, before she slept and closed her eyes on her own sound advice.

Breakfast was early; the children had to be at school by eight o'clock and Tyco left shortly after that. Charity took them to the school gates, led enthusiastically by the pair of them. She kissed them goodbye, reminded them that Nel would fetch them at noon since she was to meet their father for lunch, and hurried back to the house. It was a cold day and she had worn her winter coat and little cap and known that they didn't match up to the elegance of the other mothers escorting their children. Tyco had said that she must go shopping and her head was full of ways and means as she reached the house. Jolly opened the door to her with a note in his hand. 'The professor asked me to give you this, *mevrouw*. There is a nice fire in the little parlour, and I will bring coffee at ten o'clock if that suits you.'

The note was brief to the point of terseness. 'I will fetch you at noon or shortly after. Please be ready.'

It was a long while until noon; the morning stretched emptily before her or so she thought, but the appearance of Mrs Jolly, anxious to show her around the house, this time peering in cupboards, and inspecting the empty bedrooms thoroughly, not to mention the linen-room and the entire contents of the kitchen and its various store-rooms, filled the emptiness very nicely so that she had to hurry a little in order to be ready for Tyco.

He came a little after noon and she fancied that he eyed her critically as he kissed her cheek and enquired after her morning. Deeply conscious of her unassuming appearance, she got into the car beside him and, with Samson sitting proudly in the back, they drove to the Herengracht.

The bank was a large grey building, solidly built and very well appointed. They went at once to the manager's office and Tyco said, 'Please excuse us if we speak Dutch now and again. I'll explain everything later.'

The manager was a square, bearded man who welcomed them warmly and, after shaking Charity's hand, embarked on a brisk talk with Tyco.

Presently Tyco said, 'Will you sign your name, my dear, so that you can have your cheque-book? Your allowance is waiting for you when you need it and you will get a statement each month.'

So she did as she was asked and took the cheque-book without looking inside, although she was dying of curiosity. Only in the car once more, sitting beside Tyco, did she venture to peer inside it at the opening statement folded there.

'There's a mistake,' she told him with a gasp. 'It's more than I have ever earned in a year—I can't possibly spend it all in a year...'

'That is your quarterly allowance, Charity, just for your own use. The children have their own cheque-book—remind me to let you have it. You will need clothes.' His eyes swept briefly over her person. 'You always look nice but I should like my wife to be in the fashion—buy all the clothes you need and if you run out of money, say so.'

'If you don't mind me asking, have you a lot of money?'

He turned to look at her. 'Yes, a great deal, Charity. Perhaps I should have mentioned it.' He sounded placid and his smile was kind.

'No—no, of course not. I don't wish to be inquisitive. She added with a kind of childish glee, 'I've never had so much money before.'

He started the car and drove to Dikker en Thijs, an elegant restaurant on the Prinsengracht, where he gave her lunch.

'Shall you go shopping this afternoon?' he wanted to know.

'Well, I'll look around; perhaps I should go to a hairdresser's first.'

'Do not, I beg of you, alter your hairstyle in any way; it's very nice as it is, soft and mousy. I should much prefer you to look as you always look, but buy all the clothes you want by all means. I rather think that within a few weeks we shall receive a number of invitations for dinner—my colleagues' wives will call at teatime and later on there will be the hospital ball.' He glanced at his watch. 'I am sorry that I can't stay with you but I've a list this afternoon. Nel is taking the children back? Good.'

'Yes, but I shall fetch them at four o'clock—I said that I would.'

'I'll drop you off at the P.C. Hoofstraat; it is full of little dress shops. Reka and Fenna both go there.'

She watched him drive away before she started walking down the street, looking in the boutique windows as she went. It occurred to her that he had been very helpful, giving her some idea of the clothes she would need, telling her where to buy them. He was so kind and thoughtful; she would try to repay him by being exactly the wife he wanted.

Within minutes she had seen something she was going to buy. A top coat of superfine wool in hunter's green, beautifully cut and, she felt sure, her size.

It was, and so was a tweed suit, green and brown with a cashmere sweater to go with it ... Charity embarked on that most pleasant of occupations, buying clothes without looking at the price tags first.

CHAPTER SEVEN

CHARITY, wearing the new coat and a chic little felt hat to match it, left the boutique with the promise that the suit and the coat she had been wearing would be delivered within the hour. It had been gratifying to see that Tyco was known; indeed, the saleslady begged her to return at any time. 'Madam has a charming figure,' she enthused, 'and we shall be having our spring stock very shortly.'

I mustn't let this go to my head, reflected Charity, going from one elegant little window to the next, and before long she had bought soft leather boots, elegant shoes and two handbags and here again they would be delivered that afternoon, which left her free to search for a dress or two. A jersey three-piece in old rose caught her eye and became hers; so did a fine wool dress in a rich tawny colour. By then time was running out but there was always tomorrow, she thought happily, summoning a taxi with all the aplomb of an assured young matron.

The children fell upon her as they came out of school.

'You've got a new coat and hat,' cried Letizia. 'Have you bought anything else?' and Teile chimed in with,

'When are we going shopping with you?'

'On Saturday morning? Your Papa says you may have some new frocks...'

She had tea with them in the schoolroom and then took them to her bedroom to help her unpack the boxes which had arrived. Tyco found them there when he got home, so busy admiring the old rose three-piece that none of them saw him leaning against the door-jamb.

'A start has been made?' he asked with placid good humour, and all three of them turned to look at him. The children ran to him as they always did but Charity stayed where she was, smiling rather shyly.

He kissed his daughters and strolled across the room to where she stood. He didn't kiss her, though, only asked her if she had enjoyed her afternoon.

'Yes, oh, yes, very much. And I've brought a great deal back.'

He glanced at the clothes spread on the bed and across the chairs. 'As I said, you've made a start.'

'Yes. I thought I might take the girls shopping on Saturday morning—they need a few things.'

'By all means. I leave it entirely to you, my dear.'

Charity was surprised to find that she had slipped into her new role with such ease; of course it was made easy by Tyco's matter-of-fact approach to their marriage, his acceptance of her presence in his home as though she had been there for years instead of days. The week came to an end; a delightfully busy period for her, going each day to comb the boutiques for the right clothes. By Saturday she had acquired a collection of clothes which she hoped would cover every occasion likely to arise and was glad of it when Tyco handed her an envelope at breakfast on Saturday morning. 'Mevrouw ter Appel invites us to dine a week today—the first of many, I'm sure. We will go, of course. They are old friends.'

Presently he left for the hospital and she and the children were driven by Jolly in the Rover to La Bonneterie where they spent a delightful morning and a good deal of money and returned home to find Tyco sitting in his chair with Samson at his side, reading his post.

He expressed suitable pleasure at their successful shopping, declared that he could hardly wait to see the new dresses and suggested that they might like to go to the Opera House on the Waterlooplein that afternoon. 'Sleeping Beauty,' he continued. 'The Royal Netherlands Ballet Company are performing. I have a box, and it starts at two o'clock.'

The girls were too excited to eat much of their lunch. 'But if you both eat your pudding,' coaxed Charity 'and drink all your milk, you will have time to change into your new red dresses.' She was going to change too; the tawny wool would do very nicely...

The afternoon was a success—the two little girls sat enthralled between Charity and Tyco, speechless with delight. Charity was enthralled too. She hadn't mentioned it but she had never been to the ballet before; if she had but known it, her face bore the same absorbed wonder as the children's and Tyco smiled at the sight of it—he found it rather more to his liking than the ballet.

They all went to the English church on Sunday morning but afterwards he went to the hospital and didn't come home until after tea and then, once the children were in bed, he said that he had a good deal of work to catch up on and would Charity mind being on her own for an hour or so?

'Not in the least,' she took great care to say with just the right amount of understanding in her voice.

She hadn't really expected anything else, she told herself silently, and thanked heaven that she had had the sense to buy wool and needles for the jumpers she intended to knit for the children. The sort of jumpers Miss Bloom wouldn't have considered—Teile was to have sheep gavotting across the front of hers, and Letizia had chosen a flight of ducks. Charity, who liked knitting and was expert at it, cast on the stitches with pleasure.

She had almost finished the ribbing by the time he came back again and a few minutes later Jolly came in to say that dinner was served.

Tyco had gone to pour their drinks. 'Ask Mrs Jolly to hold everything for five minutes, will you, Jolly? I quite forgot the time.' He looked across at Charity. 'I'm sorry, my dear.'

She smiled gently, finished the row and stuck her needles in the wool. 'The time goes quickly when one is occupied; I enjoy sitting here by the fire, being lazy.'

After dinner, in case he felt that he must entertain her with chat, she became absorbed in her knitting instructions, giving him the chance to read his papers if he wished to do so.

She finished the ribbing and was weaving in the wool for the first sheep when he asked idly, 'What are you knitting, Charity?'

'Jumpers for the children.' She held up the patterns for him to see. 'They're all the fashion among the children at school, you know. Teile has the sheep and Letizia wanted ducks.'

'Clever girl. Can you cook and sew as well as make dolls' houses out of boxes?'

She wasn't sure if he were joking or not but the answered him seriously. 'Well, I can cook, but nothing like Mrs Jolly of course, and I can sew and knit; most women can.'

'The ladies of my acquaintance must be shy of allowing their talent to be seen, although my mother shares your interest in such things and Lucia is a very domesticated girl. I must say that it is most restful to sit here and watch your busy fingers.' He said to surprise her, 'We have been married a week, Charity.'

'Eight days; how time flies.'

'No regrets?' The question was casual.

'None. It's all still strange, of course, but the children are dears and Jolly and Mrs Jolly are so kind and thoughtful.' She shot him a smiling look. 'And all my lovely new clothes.'

He laughed then. 'Well, we must make opportunities for you to wear them.'

Two days later he brought Mevrouw de Groot home, explaining blandly that he had given her a lift, and by chance—a lucky one—Charity had decided to try out a particularly pretty outfit—a long pleated skirt in grey jersey, a silk blouse in pale pink and a short boxy jacket with a neat little pink pattern. While she was at it, she had got into the grey suede and kid shoes which went so well with it. The result pleased her and she set off to fetch the children from school, shrouded in the new top coat and wearing the boots. It was a raw day and they hurried home, where she discarded the coat, donned the shoes and pivoted before the little girls, as pleased as they were at her transformation.

They had gone straight into the schoolroom for their tea, for the children had some homework to do and Charity had been firm about them getting it done before their father got home, but she had barely lifted the teapot when the door opened and he came in, ushering a tall, strikingly dark woman before him.

Charity put down the teapot and looked enquiringly at Tyco, although she guessed who it was before he spoke. 'Hello, my dears—I'm home early for once and I've brought Mevrouw de Groot to meet you, Charity. She is an old friend . . .'

Is she indeed? thought Charity waspishly, and thank heaven I've got this outfit on. Her pleasantly smiling face showed nothing of her thoughts. She offered a hand and murmured politely in reply to Mevrouw de Groot's effusive greeting. She was charming to the children too but although they were on their best behaviour they showed no pleasure in her appearance. Charity wondered why they didn't like her and the thought followed hard on her wonder that she didn't like her either.

'We are having tea here because the girls have some homework to do, but Nel can come here and we can go downstairs—I'm sure you will have tea?'

'I never drink it,' declared Mevrouw de Groot, 'but you won't mind if Tyco gives me a glass of sherry before I go? Don't let me disturb your tea.' She gave a tinkling laugh. 'This isn't a visit; we just happened to—how do you say?—bump into each other.'

'You must come to tea one day soon,' said Charity. 'It is so nice to meet Tyco's friends.'

She hadn't looked at him, aware that he was leaning against the wall, looking amused. Now she said pleasantly, 'Tyco, do take Mevrouw de Groot to the drawing-room and give her that drink. Such a wretched afternoon.' She went on chattily, 'A glass of sherry will be just the thing.' She smiled at the woman and offered a hand. 'I'm so glad we have met,' she said with insincere fervour, 'and do please come again soon.'

Alone again with the children Teile said in a whispering voice, 'Charity, we don't like her. You shouldn't let Papa take her to the drawing-room; she wants to marry him—we heard Miss Bloom say so...'

Charity giggled. 'Well, she can't, my dears; Papa is married to me.'

'She won't be able to make him change his mind, will she? We like you very much.'

'I like you very much, too, and no, I don't think your papa will change his mind. Listen, my dears. Even though Papa is married to me, he may have all the friends he wants—why should he give them up? He must have known many of them long before he met me.'

She kissed the two enquiring faces. 'Now let us have our tea. There are muffins in that dish and Mrs Jolly has made a chocolate sponge especially for you both.'

They had finished the muffins and had made inroads into the sponge when Tyco came back. He cast a look at the muffin dish and observed, 'Have you eaten them all?'

'Every one,' said Charity composedly. 'I'll get Jolly to bring up some more, and another pot of tea.'

He sat down at the table, asked the little girls what they had been doing at school and demolished the muffins when they were brought.

'Homework?' he wanted to know.

When they said, 'Yes,' he said,

'I want to talk to Charity—we'll come back in half an hour and see how you are getting on. You don't mind?'

'Not if you're with Charity,' said Letizia.

'Too early for a drink?' asked Tyco, sitting down opposite Charity in the drawing-room.

'Oh, much,' she said promptly.

He grinned and then said, 'You look nice—something I haven't seen yet?'

'There are a great many things you haven't seen yet,' said Charity tartly.

He smiled a little. 'I look forward to rectifying the omission. Do you want to know anything more about Mevrouw de Groot?'

She had picked up her knitting, such a useful occupation when one was put out. 'More? I don't know anything about her...'

'I seem to remember the children—er—expressing their disapproval. You were lunching with us.'

Charity went pink. 'Oh, that—yes, well...'

He continued as though she hadn't spoken. 'She was a friend of my first wife's and when Miranda was killed she transferred her friendship to me.' He added without conceit, 'She has been trying to marry me ever since.'

'Oh, is that why you——?' Then she caught her breath and choked on the rest of the sentence.

'Married you?' He sounded very placid. 'No, certainly not. Consider, my dear; if I had wanted to escape her clutches I could have married at any time during the past few years. To tell the truth I never gave the matter much thought. I had Miss Bloom for the children and I had—still have—my work, but when I met you it seemed to me that you would fill the empty place in my home. The children love you, I have never seen them so happy and content, and I— I find you a most restful person; it is as though you have been there all the time, you fit in so well.'

Charity said, 'Oh!' and couldn't think of anything else to say.

He added deliberately 'Young van Kamp's loss is my gain.'

'He never really had me to lose,' she said quietly. 'When you're a plain girl like me you're likely to get carried away when someone tells you you are the only girl in the world; you want to believe him and you make all kinds of excuses. It hurts but I dare say it's good for you.'

He got up, came across to her chair and hauled her gently to her feet. 'To be hurt is never good for anyone, and why it had to happen to someone as kind and gentle as you I do not know. Promise me something, Charity. If you are unhappy or sad, will you tell me? You are so much younger than I am and I have only just realised that. Should you meet a man more your own age and love him you must tell me— any man for that matter.'

He put a hand under her chin so that she had to look at him. 'Promise?'

'I promise. Will you do the same, Tyco?'

'I? My dear girl, I rather believe that I am immune to romance, but I'll promise.' He bent and kissed her, not on the cheek this time.

It was a gentle kiss but it sent a pleasant thrill through her person; she kissed him back shyly. She drew back a little. 'Thank you for telling me about Mevrouw de Groot, but you didn't have to, you know.'

He ran a finger down her cheek. 'No secrets,' he said, and smiled again. She really looked rather pretty; mousy hair had its own unobtrusive beauty and her eyes were lovely. 'We had better see how those children are getting on.'

January merged stormily into February and Charity, after one or two false starts, settled down into her new life. The children had accepted her happily and she was fond of them and enjoyed their company. Mrs Jolly had tactfully handed over several household duties—the flowers, the ordering of the meals, even the occasional shopping when something special was needed. Her days were agreeably filled, for invitations came thick and fast and, hard on their heels, the various wives of Tyco's friends came for coffee or tea. Charity, who had been dreading meeting them, found them more than kind, full of helpful advice, anxious to make her feel at home with them. The dinner parties she had secretly dreaded turned out to be unexpectedly entertaining and Tyco, without appearing to do so, was always there at her elbow. She wore the pretty dresses she had bought, anxious to look her best, and the diamond earrings he had given her as a wedding present. She had been delighted with them, at the same time suppressing the doubt that he had quite forgotten to give her anything until he had noticed the simple chain bracelet which his mother had given her. She had opened the box when they had got home from their visit to his family and found it nestling in its bed of blue satin, and for quite a time she hadn't worn it in case he had thought that she was reminding him deliberately of his forgetfulness but then one afternoon he had come back early, and she had put it on because it went well with the dress she was wearing.

She had told him when he had asked her who had given it to her and the day after he had given her the earrings.

It was on a cold dreary day while she and the children were having tea in the schoolroom that he came home earlier than usual and joined them for a meal, and, as usual, without her fully realising it, Charity sighed with the pleasure of seeing him again. She poured his tea, offered toast and sat quietly listening to the little girls giving him an account of their day. He listened patiently, and when they paused took a letter from his pocket. 'This came for you at the hospital,' he told her as he handed it to her and turned his attention back to the twins.

Charity knew the writing—Eunice's. She hadn't written since Charity had come to Holland and the letter Charity had sent telling her of her marriage had been returned with 'Gone Away' scrawled across it.

Tyco glanced at her. 'Do read it, my dear.'

She smiled at him and opened it. The letter was short, to say that Eunice had a modelling engagement in Amsterdam and would be there for a week. She gave the dates—she would be arriving in a day's time and intended telephoning the hospital. 'Though I doubt if we shall see much of each other; I'm swamped with invitations.'

Charity folded the letter and put it back in the envelope. 'It's from Eunice; she's coming to Amsterdam—she will be here tomorrow but she doesn't say when. She says she'll ring the hospital.'

'Of course, she thinks you are still there. She must come here unless she has made arrangements already. How shall we let her know?' He paused. 'Shall I ask the switchboard to put any calls for you through to me? I can give her our address and she can come when she wishes. Is she on holiday?'

'No, modelling. I expect that takes up a good deal of her day. But I would like to see her. You don't mind if she comes here—to tea, perhaps, or lunch?'

'My dear Charity, she is most welcome to stay here.' He spoke very kindly and she smiled her gratitude.

'I should like to be a model,' said Teile. 'Is she very pretty, your sister?'

'My stepsister. Yes, she is, very.'

'You're not pretty,' said Letizia, 'but you've got a very nice face and you smile a lot. Is that because you are happy with us?'

Charity nodded. 'Yes, I'm very happy, dear. You'll like meeting Eunice; she will tell you all about modelling. It's very hard work, you know.'

'Then I shall change my mind,' said Teile, instantly, 'I'll marry a millionaire and have six children.'

Tyco laughed. 'They're quite hard work, too, but they're worth it, aren't they, Charity?'

He passed his cup for more tea. 'We are home this evening, aren't we? Good, an hour or so by the fire with the papers and you and your knitting for company is exactly what I need. We might even watch television for half an hour.'

Which was exactly what they did. He with Samson at his feet and newspapers strewn around his chair and she with her knitting and a head full of vague troubled thoughts. There was nothing to trouble her, she reflected, so why did she have this sad uncertain feeling? Life was good, she told herself, and Tyco was kind and considerate; he liked her, too, she knew that. Only, she thought sadly, he wasn't interested in her as a woman. She was his companion, someone to be at home when he got back after a hard day, to sit at the foot of his table and be hostess to all the other doctors' wives and, above all, to be as good a substitute mother for the twins as she could manage. She should be content and very nearly was, but if only he would notice her as a person. He was punctilious in admiring her dresses when she wore something new but he didn't look at her...

'You are knitting like one of the furies,' said Tyco pleasantly. 'What's the matter, Charity?'

She hadn't known that he had been watching her for some minutes. She smiled at once. 'The matter? Nothing. I've got to a difficult bit and I want to get it over as quickly as possible.'

'You aren't worried about your stepsister coming?'

'No, of course not. She will be surprised...'

He said kindly, 'I look forward to meeting her. I shall be late tomorrow, by the way; there's a consultants' meeting at five o'clock.'

'The children are having the van Erp girls round for tea; I'm bringing them back when I fetch the girls and someone will fetch them at six o'clock.'

'Good. They're happy, aren't they?'

'I think so. They're doing so well at school.'

She didn't enlarge on that, for he had cast down the paper he was reading and got to his feet. 'I must just phone the hospital and then dictate some letters on to a tape ready for tomorrow.' He bent over her and touched her cheek lightly. 'Goodnight, Charity.'

She said goodnight cheerfully, aware that he was still looking at her intently.

She took care to be cheerful at breakfast too. He didn't get home until after seven o'clock that evening; she was in the drawing-room with the children on either side of her while she read *Little Women* to them and he paused in the doorway to look at them. Sitting there, with the girls curled up against her, the soft glow from the reading lamp lighting up her mousy hair and the soft blue of her dress, Charity looked charming. She paused, and they all laughed at something she had read and looked up and saw him there. She felt the colour rush into her cheeks and a sudden delight at the sight of him which took her by surprise, for there was nothing different in his usually placid expression. She said with unwonted briskness, 'Here is your papa...' and sat quietly while they ran to kiss him.

He came over to her and put a hand on her shoulder. 'Your stepsister telephoned as we expected and they put the call through to me. She had just arrived and naturally enough was surprised to hear that you were married. I told her our address and she will call to see you, probably not tomorrow but certainly on the day after.'

'Oh, good.' She spoke cheerfully, and all the while she wished most fervently that Eunice weren't coming.

They were dining out that evening; a rather grand occasion with the *burgermeester* as guest of honour, and what with getting the little girls to their beds and changing into one of her new dresses she had little time to think about Eunice. She had given much thought to what she would wear: honey-coloured chiffon over a silk slip with a full skirt, simply cut. She hoped that it would do justice to the occasion and went downstairs to join Tyco feeling rather uncertain about it. His smile of appreciation put her doubts as rest. 'Exactly right,' he observed in his kind way. 'You have unerring good taste, my dear.'

He picked up a jewellers' box from the table beside him. 'Perhaps you will wear this; my grandmother left it to me in the hope that I would give it to my wife some day.' He saw her questioning look. 'Some years after Miranda was killed,' he added blandly. 'Grandmother died last year and I am sorry that you never knew her or she you. You would have got on famously.'

He had opened the box and lifted out a double string of pearls with a diamond clasp.

'They're beautiful . . .'

'And very old—I've had them restrung.'

He turned her round, fastened the pearls around her throat and stood back to look at her. 'Quite perfect, you will have our *burgermeester* eating out of your hand.'

Much to her astonishment she found that she did. He was a nice old man, very dignified as befitted his office, but he spoke excellent English and had a lively sense of humour. By the time she and Tyco were home again she was in a pleasant glow of satisfaction; she had felt at ease with the other guests and they had been friendly and, best of all, Tyco was pleased with her. Perhaps even a little proud of her. She hoped so, and went happily to bed.

He wasn't at breakfast. Jolly met her with the news that he had been sent for in the early hours of the morning—there had been a bad fire in the city and there were several badly burned victims. 'I was to say that he might be gone all day *mevrouw*, and if you would like to see Mrs Jolly presently so that she could cook a dinner that wouldn't spoil.'

'Yes, of course, I'll come as soon as I've taken the children to school. Luckily we aren't going out this evening.'

It was after seven o'clock that evening before he got home. Knowing that he would be tired, she had coaxed the children to have their baths and be ready for bed before their supper and once they had greeted him they went cheerfully enough upstairs, with the promise that they would be tucked up presently.

Tyco didn't say that he was tired but his face was lined with fatigue.

'Sit down,' said Charity briskly. 'Would you like a drink or coffee?'

'A drink—a strong one. I showered at the hospital but I wanted to come home.'

He smiled at her and she said warmly, 'You've had a dreadful day, haven't you? Was it very bad? Do you want to talk about it?'

She gave him his drink and poured herself a glass of sherry.

'How fortunate I am to come home to a wife who is willing to listen and, what is more, understand what I am telling her. Yes. It has been a bad day. Six— three very serious—third-degree burns—all children. The fourth child will do, and so will the mother and father. Zuster Kingsma was magnificent—they all were, and Wim is a splendid colleague.'

'You're still worried about the three children?'

'Yes—specially the youngest, a mere two years old.' He began to tell her about it and she listened carefully until Jolly came to tell them that dinner was served.

'First we must go and say goodnight to the children,' said Tyco, and took her arm as they went upstairs to the bedroom the girls shared.

He had been hungry; Charity was glad that she and Mrs Jolly had put their heads together and decided on just the kind of meal a tired man might eat;

vichyssoise, tarragon chicken and a bread and butter pudding such as only Mrs Jolly could make. She had gone to the cellars too with Jolly, something she would never normally do, and on his advice had chosen a white burgundy. '1983 vintage,' Jolly had told her. 'An excellent wine.'

Charity, who knew nothing about wines, but intended to learn fast, took his word for it.

Back in the drawing-room they sat over their coffee, not talking much, she with her knitting—the sheep were finished; she was busy with the ducks now—and he with the day's news. We must look like an old married couple, reflected Charity, content to sit together, hardly speaking but still needing each other. She sighed, and looked across at Tyco and found him watching her. Once again she had the agreeable sensation of pleasure, unable to look away from him.

Tyco threw his paper down. 'Charity——' He was interrupted by Jolly.

'Miss Pearson has called to see *mevrouw*,' he stated in his dignified way.

'Ah, your stepsister,' said Tyco and got up as Eunice came in.

Charity got up too and the pair of them watched as Eunice crossed the room to them. She stopped halfway and flung out her arms in a rather dramatic fashion. 'Charity, just how did you manage it? You of all people getting married.' Her lovely eyes took in Tyco's good looks. 'And to my ideal man, too.' She laughed then and kissed Charity with a good deal more warmth than Charity would have expected and then turned to Tyco.

'This is Tyco, Eunice. Tyco, my stepsister,' said Charity, feeling somehow stuffy. Until that moment she had been feeling rather pleased with herself; her dress was pretty, she was nicely made up, her hair, simply dressed, shone with cleanliness, and yet suddenly she felt dowdy.

Eunice was enough to make anyone feel like that; her golden hair was arranged artlessly around her lovely face, her make-up was expertly done and her clothes were in the extreme of fashion: the briefest of skirts, a kind of cloak, dramatic in black velvet, thrown carelessly over one shoulder, which she threw off on to a chair, and a suede waistcoat over a chiffon blouse. Eye-catching, thought Charity waspishly, and Tyco's eyes were caught...

'Do sit down,' she said cheerfully. 'I'll ring for coffee. Have you had a busy day?'

Eunice sat down close to Tyco. 'Oh, lord, yes, and I'd love coffee—I'd like a whisky too...'

Tyco got her drink and sat down again, his face placidly welcoming, and when the coffee came Charity poured it while Eunice watched with an impish grin. 'I can't believe my eyes,' she said, and looked at Tyco. 'Are you something important? You were in the hospital when I phoned?'

'I work there. Where are you staying?'

'Oh, at the Hilton—a boring place; I'm here for five days—for the dress shows, you know.' She smiled across at Charity. 'If I stay a couple of days longer may I come here? I want to see something of the town and I could do with a break.'

'Of course you may. We'll be delighted, won't we, Tyco?'

'Certainly. The children will love to see a real live model——'

'Children?' Just for a moment Eunice looked nonplussed.

'I have twin daughters by my first wife,' said Tyco smoothly. 'They're devoted to Charity.'

'So you're a stepmother!' Eunice laughed. 'Let's hope you make a better job of it than Mother made with you.' She glanced at Tyco. 'They never hit it off, my mother and Charity.'

He said gently. 'You do not live with your mother? You visit her frequently, perhaps?'

Eunice shrugged. 'Well, no. We don't get on awfully well—she likes to live in France and I'm much in demand.' She cast him a smiling glance. 'But if I could find someone like you I'd settle down.' Her eyes roved round the lovely room. 'You live in style, don't you?' She laughed again. 'You've fallen on your feet, Charity.'

She was outrageous, thought Charity, but so lovely to look at that she would be forgiven for anything she said or did. Tyco had looked at her several times and it struck Charity that the peculiar feeling in her insides was jealousy. Ridiculous, she told herself severely; your own stepsister and she'll be gone in a week. Out loud she said calmly, 'I'm very happy. Amsterdam is a lovely place in which to live and I'm making a lot of friends. Are you living in London still?'

'Off and on.' Eunice turned to Tyco again; it was a waste of time to talk to Charity when this quiet handsome man was there to be charmed.

She stayed till late and when at last she got up to go she said airily, 'I'll pop in whenever I'm free for an hour or two.' She flipped her eyelashes at Tyco. 'After all, I am family, aren't I?'

'We shall be delighted,' he told her blandly, and Charity, not to be outdone, chimed in,

'Yes, please do come.'

It sounded inadequate and Eunice threw her a mocking glance as she went to the door. Sure of getting what she wanted, she had asked Tyco to ferry her back to the hotel and he had complied with what Charity crossly considered to be unnecessary willingness. The Hilton was some way from the centre of the city and it was late. She saw them off with smiles and hand waving and then went back to wait for Tyco to return. They could have called a taxi at that time of night.

Jolly came to clear away the tray and she told him to go to bed. 'You will have locked up?' she asked him. 'If the professor wants anything I can get it; I'll wait up for him and he will lock the door when he comes in.'

It seemed a long time before she heard Tyco go past the house to the garage. She gave the dying fire a poke and picked up her knitting once more. When he came into the room she said, 'Thank you for taking Eunice back—you must be so tired.'

He stood looking at her. 'Oh, I am. She is very stimulating company, isn't she?' He strolled over to his chair. 'And quite lovely.'

Charity held down a wish to fling her knitting at his head and then went quite pale at the very idea. Eunice was lovely, he was quite right, and she was fun...

She looked at him, sitting there, weary to his bones, his eyes closed. He looked every minute of his age; he had said that he was too old for her, but he wasn't— he was just right and she had just discovered that she was in love with him.

CHAPTER EIGHT

THE shock of it made Charity feel quite peculiar. Her heart was thumping like a steam hammer and breathing had become difficult, but she made an effort to behave normally. 'Would you like more coffee?' she asked him. 'I sent Jolly to bed; he's locked up . . .'

'Eunice is even more reviving than coffee. How is it possible that you can be stepsisters? But of course you are not related in actual fact, are you?'

'No,' snapped Charity, and softened that by adding, 'She must have found it very dull when she and my stepmother came to live with us.'

'She is making up for that now, I imagine—she must lead a very colourful life.'

'Oh, yes. I'm—I'm glad you liked her.' She almost choked on her own words.

'I find her fascinating,' said Tyco.

'Oh, good.' She couldn't think of anything else to say so she murmured something about being tired, wished him goodnight in a brisk manner and went to her room, where she gave vent to her feelings by throwing a pillow or two on to the floor, having a good cry and then lying for far too long in a very hot bath. If this was being in love then it was a very unsettling business; with hindsight she saw now that her infatuation for Cor had borne not the least resemblance to the strong feelings she now knew. The possibilities of forbidding Eunice to cross the threshold, rushing downstairs and telling Tyco that she couldn't possibly live without him, or, alternatively, leaving the house forever, chased each other round and round inside her head, making an utter confusion. She crept into bed with the beginnings of a headache so that she slept badly, and got herself out of bed heavy-eyed and leaden-footed in the morning.

Her wan appearance was seized upon the moment she entered the children's room, ready to brush hair and advise on what to wear.

'You look as though you've been crying,' said Teile anxiously.

'I expect I've caught a cold. Hurry up, love, or Papa will have finished his breakfast.'

Her dread at seeing him again was needless. He wished her his usual placid good morning, remarked on the cheerless weather, reminded her that they were dining with the ter Appels that evening and embarked on a discussion about the school play with his daughters. It was just as he was on the point of leaving that Letizia said, 'Charity's got a cold—her eyes are all puffy.'

'Ah, I wondered if that was the reason.' He came round to her chair and bent to look at her. 'Do you think you will be all right for tonight, or shall I cancel it?'

'No, no.' She sounded panicky. 'I shall be quite all right, really.'

'Good. I'll do my best to get home early.' He patted her shoulder and she didn't look up. If she had done so she would have seen a gleam in his eyes, part amusement, part something else.

When she got back at lunchtime with the children, it was to find Eunice sitting in the drawing-room, a glass in her hand.

'Oh, hello, Charity. I told Jolly you had asked me to lunch—you don't mind? I've a couple of hours to spare and I'm dying to get to know that husband of yours.' Her eyes lighted on the two little girls. 'Are these the children?'

'Letizia and Teile,' answered Charity. 'They come home for lunch each day. Tyco stays at the hospital.'

'Just my rotten luck.' She nodded carelessly at the children, who were staring at her, their eyes round. 'Well, I could miss a party this evening, I suppose, and spend it with you.'

'We're dining out with one of the professors and his wife.'

Eunice shrugged. 'How dreary. Anyway, I've two more days' work then I'm free and you did invite me to stay.' She gave Charity a malicious glance. 'Though I'm not sure that you want me...'

'You are very welcome,' said Charity untruthfully. 'Run and wash your hands for lunch, my dears, and come straight down to the dining-room.' When they had gone, still wordless, she took off her coat and hat, went back into the hall and laid them on a chair and then went back to Eunice. 'Shall we have lunch? The children have to be back at school by half-past one.'

Eunice followed her into the dining-room. 'You live in style, don't you? Pots of money, I suppose—you sly creature, Charity, how did you do it?' She took the chair Jolly pulled out for her. 'He can't be in love with you...'

It was fortunate that the children joined them and there was no need to answer. Charity, conscious of Jolly's fatherly presence, launched herself on a series of questions about Eunice's job which kept that young lady busy for the whole of the meal. As they left the dining-room she asked, 'Which way are you going? We might as well walk together if you're going our way...'

Jolly had heard her; he offered Eunice her coat to clinch the matter.

'Oh, well, there's no point in my staying,' said Eunice. 'I can get a taxi from the end of the street, I suppose?'

'Easily,' Charity spoke cheerfully. 'I do hope you enjoy your party.'

They parted on the pavement, going in opposite directions, and Teile said, 'I don't like her and nor does Letizia, do you Letizia?'

'No, she didn't shake hands, and she laughs too much when it isn't funny.'

Charity agreed with silent fervour, but all she said was, 'Well, she leads a very glamorous life, you know, with lots of pretty clothes and friends.'

'You've got friends and pretty clothes too and you're not a bit like her,' said Teile.

'Well, I'm not pretty, my dears. I dare say when you're as lovely as Eunice, you get used to being admired and—and...' She paused and Teile finished for her,

'And having your own way.'

'Perhaps.' She stooped to kiss the two small faces and then watched them run into the school, turned with a sigh and went back home.

The children were ready for bed and she was dressed ready to go out when Tyco got home. She was wearing a silvery grey dress with long tight sleeves and a slim skirt, and it gave her an unwonted air of elegance.

'I do like that,' he said, looking up from hugging his daughters. 'Is your cold better, my dear?'

'I don't think it is a cold, just early morning stuffiness. Have you had a very busy day again?'

He nodded, but before he could say anything more Teile said urgently, 'Papa, Eunice invited herself for lunch—we didn't ask her, she just came while we were coming home from school. She wanted to see you, she said.'

'I'm flattered. Now off to bed, *liefjes*. Charity and I mustn't be late for our dinner party; I'd better change—give me fifteen minutes.'

He went away and she saw the children into their beds and then went to sit in the drawing-room, the picture of serenity—which she wasn't—and she pondered Eunice's visit. A couple of days, she had said, but, knowing her stepsister, the two days could be stretched to a week. She sat staring into the fire and Tyco, coming in, observed, 'You're looking sad. Is anything the matter?'

'No, nothing.' She thought wildly for the right answer. 'I was thinking about tomorrow's meals.'

She blushed as she spoke, because it was a silly excuse that he probably would not believe. He didn't, but he said nothing, only smiled at her as he sat down in his chair. 'Ten minutes before we need to leave,' he observed, and closed his eyes.

He came home for lunch the following day, something which she hadn't expected. The dull day became all at once full of promise, a promise to be wiped out

by his observation over lunch that Eunice had telephoned the hospital and invited herself for dinner that
evening. 'I'll pick her up when I leave the hospital,'
he went on. 'We should be home about six o'clock.'

'How very nice,' said Charity insincerely. He turned
to speak to Teile and she cast him a loving look; it
was wistful, too.

It was half-past six before they arrived that evening.
The children were just about to have their supper in
the schoolroom and she had nipped away to change
into something which had a chance of competing with
Eunice's appearance. She got into a silk jersey dress,
made short work of her face and hair and went back
to the schoolroom. She hadn't been there five minutes
before Jolly came to tell her that the professor was
home and the young lady with him and would she
join them in the drawing-room.

Tyco was in his chair and Eunice was sitting on its
arm, swinging a leg and laughing. He got up as she
went in and crossed the room and kissed her; not his
usual peck but lingering and light, and she smiled up
at him with the delight of it before greeting Eunice.

Eunice said hello in a sulky voice. 'I've had a ghastly
day—one show after the other. You have no idea how
tired I am. One more day . . . I can't wait to come and
stay with you.'

Tyco was pouring drinks. 'Well, we don't lead a
very exciting life, you know, but we're quite central
if you want to do some sightseeing.'

Eunice pouted. 'I can't sightsee on my own. I was
counting on you to show me around, Tyco.'

He handed her a glass. 'I'm a working man, Eunice,
but Charity knows all of Amsterdam quite well now;

she can take you to the museums and churches that you will want to see.'

'Oh, she will be far too busy looking after the house and children.'

'Er—not as busy as all that,' he answered mildly, and smiled across at Charity. 'Are we promised to anyone for the next day or so?'

'Dinner with the van Tromps the day after tomorrow; Wim's wife is coming for coffee and one or two others—oh, and the children have their art exhibition...'

'Ah, yes. We must go to that without fail.'

Eunice got off the chair and wandered round the room, looking at the portraits on its walls. 'Well, if you can find time to look at a lot of childish drawings you can find a teeny-weeny hour or two to take me out.' She gave Tyco a bewitching smile. 'To a night-club perhaps. I love dancing.'

'My dancing days are over,' said Tyco suavely; a remark which made Charity blink. Only a few nights ago they had danced together after dining with some friends of his who had thrown back the rugs and invited their guests to dance to some of the latest tapes. He had exhibited no signs of middle age then and he had danced to perfection...

The memory cheered her enormously; she was beginning to think that Eunice was having it all her own way. Her satisfaction was short-lived.

'Oh, well, I'm not surprised; Charity was always a flop at parties. Still, she'll be splendid at looking after the kids, I dare say.'

'Indeed she is.' His voice was quiet but it had an edge to it. 'She is also much sought after in our circle of friends. Now I will go and see how Teile and Letizia

are—it's their bedtime.' He looked across at Charity.
'You will be up presently, darling?' he asked
deliberately...

'Ten minutes,' said Charity happily; he had called
her darling although it had only been for Eunice's
benefit.

'I shall come tomorrow,' said Eunice when he had
gone. 'I'm in no hurry to go back; I can pick and
choose for whom I'll work now.'

'That's nice,' said Charity mildly. 'You must see a
lot of the world.'

'It's boring after a while, and I'm fed up with my
men friends—they're all so young.' She glanced at
Charity. 'I think I'll have a shot at annexing Tyco—
it shouldn't be too difficult.'

'You can always try,' said Charity serenely. Her insides shook at the mere possibility; Eunice was so
beautiful and she had learned to be charming, a
dangerous combination. She stood up. 'I'll just go up
and make sure the children are in bed. Do give yourself
another drink if you want one. We shan't be long.'

Tyco was sitting cross-legged on Teile's bed with a
small daughter on either side of him and they were
all laughing as she went in.

'I'm being told about this art exhibition,' he said.
'We're to be there at three o'clock sharp and you are
to wear that hat we all like, and, for some reason
which I am unable to fathom, high heels.'

Charity sat down on Letizia's bed, facing them. 'I
know—the brown leather with the petersham bows.
They are very smart, but I teeter a bit.'

'I'll hold you up; we mustn't disappoint the
children. Unless some really dire emergency crops up,

my dears, Charity and I will be there to admire everything.'

'Don't let Eunice come,' said Letizia in a small voice. 'She laughs a lot, but it is never funny.'

'Oh, I'm sure she won't come,' said Charity comfortably, 'and she only laughs at different things from us—you see, she's very—very fashionable and witty...' She had to stop and explain what witty was. 'You see, we aren't all the same; I dare say we laugh at things which don't amuse her at all.'

'We're sorry,' said Teile, 'but we don't like her, Charity.'

'She is a guest in our house, *liefjes*,' said Tyco, 'so please remember that.'

Teile didn't give up easily. 'Do you like her, Papa?'

'She is a beautiful and charming young lady; I should imagine that she never lacks for dates.' It was an evasive answer and didn't satisfy Charity at all. The children said their prayers, got into bed, were kissed goodnight, and tucked in. When Charity and Tyco had gone, Teile said quietly, 'All the same, I hate her. Don't you, Letizia?'

'Yes. She's coming to stay...'

Eunice stayed late again. She had subtly changed her image, though. She was soft-voiced and there were no snide remarks. She evinced great interest in the hospital and wanted to know just what Tyco did. 'Of course, Charity did quite well when she trained,' she observed. 'You must miss her working for you.'

'No, not really,' said Tyco blandly. 'I have her at home instead, which is so very much nicer.'

He might not mean it but it did Charity's heart good to hear it. All the same she wasn't happy about Eunice's sudden niceness. It didn't ring true somehow, but she had no doubt that it might prove irresistible. Tyco had said that she was stimulating company; now she was being all admiration, fluttering eyelashes and gentle smiles, not forgetting her almost motherly attitude to Charity. It wasn't just motherly either, it held pity as well. 'I must say you're coping marvellously, Charity,' said Eunice with just the right amount of doubt in her voice.

Charity smiled, because there really wasn't an answer to that.

Tyco drove Eunice back to the hotel—it was a foregone conclusion that he would—and when he got back he made the disquieting remark that Eunice was probably hiding a sweet nature under her superficial manner.

Charity agreed, otherwise he might think that she was being a bit malicious. She did her best to say so with suitable mildness but she sounded snappy all the same.

There was no sign of Eunice on the following day but the day after that she phoned to say that she would be coming that evening.

'Make it the day after,' said Charity briskly. 'We have to go out this evening. I'll expect you for lunch shall I? The day after tomorrow.'

She put the phone down quickly; it was much easier to be firm on the telephone. Perhaps she had been rather terse, she thought uneasily, and, when Tyco came home, told him about it. 'I hope I didn't sound inhospitable,' she said worriedly, 'I don't mean to be, but we couldn't take her with us this evening and I'm sure she wouldn't want to be alone all evening...'

Tyco was at his most soothing. 'Don't worry, Charity; I'm sure she will understand—we'll take her out to dinner to make up for it. She will have to be on her own tomorrow afternoon, won't she? While we are at the art exhibition.'

They said no more about it, but separated to change and go to the supper party. What little time there was before they left was taken up by the children and on their return Tyco told her that he had some work to do and wished her goodnight. 'You look very nice in that outfit,' he told her, and kissed her cheek briefly.

She went to bed a prey to any number of doubts and worrying thoughts, most of them highly exaggerated and all of them difficult to pin down to a level of common sense. In broad daylight they seemed silly, especially as Eunice telephoned to say that she wouldn't be coming until the evening.

The children were to have lunch at school the next day so that they could prepare the exhibition. Charity entertained several acquaintances to coffee, ate a quick lunch herself and dressed with care, anxious to satisfy the little girls. She was waiting when Tyco got home.

'I hope I look like all the others,' she told him anxiously. 'Children do mind...'

'You look exactly right. I see that you are wearing the shoes...' he smiled at her from a tired face '...and the hat.'

'You've had a busy morning; something went wrong?'

'Not wrong, but rather more difficult than I had expected. I'll tell you about it later.'

The school courtyard was crammed with cars and parents, many of whom they knew, exchanging scraps of gossip as they went into the school hall to view the children's work. Some of it was very good, some of it rather startling. Teile had painted a house surrounded by a colourful garden of improbable flowers, and Letizia had done a pen and ink drawing of Charity and her father. They were standing arm in arm, resembling a pair of matchstick people with black dots for eyes and upturned mouths. Charity was wearing a hat. It was a child's drawing, unskilled, and yet it conveyed an impression of closeness. Charity found herself blushing for no reason at all and Tyco's glance turned into a thoughtful stare.

Letizia was hopping from one foot to the other with excitement. 'It's like you, isn't it?' she wanted to know anxiously. 'And Teile drew a house like ours for you to live in—with us of course, and some babies.'

'We like it very much,' said Tyco warmly, 'and what a very nice idea, drawing us together and giving us such a nice house.'

'They're the very best drawings in the whole room,' said Charity. 'Shall we be allowed to have them?'

'Yes, yes, you can frame them and hang them in the drawing-room.' So presently they all went home, the drawings clutched by the children, and Tyco stayed for tea before going back to the hospital. 'And I'll probably be rather late back, my dear; don't wait dinner after eight o'clock, I'll get a sandwich...'

'There will be something for you when you come in,' said Charity in a wifely voice. 'A gobbled sandwich won't go far.' She added slowly, 'Eunice will be here.'

He nodded, kissed his children, patted her shoulder in an avuncular fashion and went on his way.

Eunice arrived an hour later, bringing with her an astonishing amount of luggage. Jolly and the cabby carried it in and stacked it in the lobby and Charity, eyeing it, said doubtfully, 'You won't need more than a case or two will you, while you are here? If you tell Jolly which ones he'll take them to your room.'

'How can I possibly tell?' Eunice sounded impatient. 'I might stay quite a while...' She gave a little laugh. 'It rather depends on Tyco...'

Charity, a mild-tempered girl, boiled silently. 'Well, not really,' she said. 'You see, Tyco's family are coming to visit us at the end of the week—it's his birthday and we simply haven't room for you, Eunice.'

'Rubbish—a house this size...'

'His parents, three sisters, two brothers, quite a few children, a couple of nannies, not to mention us. You did say a couple of days, Eunice.'

'You'll have to do something. Anyway, I'll ask Tyco myself. Where is he?'

'At the hospital—he'll be late home.' Charity ignored Eunice's ill-humour. 'Come upstairs and see the children.'

Later, the children in their beds, she went downstairs to find Eunice in the drawing-room in a black silk sheath which stopped well above her knees and held in place by shoe-string shoulder-straps. She would have looked delightful in *Vogue* but in the comfortable, splendidly furnished drawing-room where the furniture had not been changed for a couple of hundred years she looked out of place.

She glanced at the clock as Charity went in. 'Tyco isn't back yet?' As she spoke the telephone rang and Charity went to answer it.

It was Tyco—to say that he wouldn't be back for another two hours at least. 'A little girl,' he told her, 'wearing one of those inflammable nighties and standing too near a gas fire; third-degree burns—

about thirty per cent, I should think. Don't wait up. Is Eunice there?'

'Yes. How dreadful, Tyco. I hope she'll be all right——'

'We shall do all that we can.'

He rang off and Eunice asked, 'Who was that?'

'Tyco. They're just admitting a badly burned child; he won't be home for hours.'

'Surely there is someone else to do the work? He knows I'm here, doesn't he?'

Charity bit back outrage. 'Yes. Will you have a drink before we have dinner?'

'Aren't we going to wait for him?'

'No. He will probably stay the night if the child is very ill.'

So dinner was eaten in a sulky silence on Eunice's part while Charity made polite conversation and took no notice. It was a relief when the meal was finished and they went back to the drawing-room for their coffee. Eunice seemed reluctant to talk so Charity turned on the television but since the programme was a lecture about the third world by a Dutch politician it hardly helped towards the evening's entertainment.

'This is boring,' declared Eunice crossly. 'What a dull life you lead—kids to look after and a husband who's never home. I'm going to bed.'

Charity stayed by the fire knitting the last of the ducks but when the clock struck eleven and Jolly came to see if she needed anything further she told him to go to bed. She went herself to her room to creep downstairs half an hour later in her dressing-gown and slippers, go to the kitchen and make sure that there was a tray laid in case Tyco did come home.

Which he did shortly after midnight, by which time she was dozing by the last of the drawing-room fire. She woke as he went into the hall and went to meet him, her hair a soft cloud around her shoulders, her face rosy with sleep.

'There you are,' she said in a motherly voice. 'Is everything all right?'

He tossed his coat on to a chair. 'I hope so; we have done our best. You should be in bed.'

She ignored that. 'Come down to the kitchen; there's soup and coffee and sandwiches. I'll make you toast if you would rather...'

He threw an arm round her and she trembled so that he said, 'You're cold, I'll see to myself, my dear.'

She took no notice of that either. In the kitchen she set a bowl of soup before him, poured coffee and uncovered the sandwiches.

He hadn't stopped to eat, he told her between mouthfuls; the treatment for the child had been too urgent. He told her about it and she listened quietly, understanding what he was talking about, knowing that just to talk it over would help him to relax. He was tired but not too tired to ask if the children were all right and if her evening had been pleasant.

She collected the dishes and carried them to the sink; Mrs Jolly or Nel would put them in the machine in the morning. 'The children went to sleep at once after all the excitement. Eunice was disappointed that you weren't home...!'

He yawned. 'I expect you had a pleasant gossip.' He caught her by the arm. 'Bed, my dear.'

They went up the staircase together and parted at the top. He took her hand in his. 'Thank you,

Charity—I had forgotten how pleasant it is to come home to someone.'

Eunice wasn't at breakfast and Tyco had been gone an hour or more before she came downstairs, looking like a fashion plate and very peevish.

'Whatever time do you have breakfast?' she wanted to know. 'Not that I ever have any...'

'About half-past seven. Tyco goes soon after eight o'clock and I take the children to school by half-past.'

'Did he come back last night?'

'Yes. Very late. I hope you slept well; were you warm enough?'

'Yes. Are we going out this evening?'

'I don't know. If Tyco feels he can leave the unit he'll let me know.'

They were having coffee when he came in. Charity stayed where she was in her chair and said, 'How nice—just in time for coffee,' but Eunice rushed across the room and flung her arms round his neck.

'No one told me what time you had breakfast,' she grumbled prettily, 'but now you're here—do tell, are we going out this evening?'

'Perhaps, but I'm not promising anything.' He had disentangled himself gently and gone to drop a kiss on Charity's cheek. 'I've given myself an hour off— I'll collect the children and drop them off on my way back.'

Jolly came in with fresh coffee and Tyco sat down in his chair with Samson draped over his feet. 'I'm sorry that I wasn't here to welcome you, Eunice,' he observed pleasantly. 'But I'm sure Charity and the children looked after you well.'

Eunice arranged one long leg over the other. 'I was so disappointed. And now Charity tells me that I can only stay for a couple of days because your family are coming to stay here for your birthday.'

If Tyco was surprised at this interesting bit of news he concealed it very well. His placid expression didn't alter one jot and nor did he look at Charity, who had gone a little pale because she had forgotten to tell him what she had said.

'I have a large family. I expect Charity told you; I have nephews and nieces as well with their nannies—the house will be packed to the roof.'

'If they stay only for one night...' began Eunice.

'A week at least,' went on Tyco, thoroughly enjoying himself. 'Most of them come from Friesland and it's a splendid chance for us to meet and exchange news.'

'Well, you must take me out this evening and tomorrow as well. I want to go to a night-club—I've a gorgeous dress I'm dying to wear.'

'Most inviting. I'll see if I can hunt up a fourth.'

'I meant just us two,' coaxed Eunice. 'Charity won't mind, will you?' She barely glanced at her. 'There's a marvellous disco, the Mazzo—can we go there?'

'We can, but we won't,' said Tyco calmly. 'We might dine out this evening...' he looked at Charity, '...if you can arrange things with Mrs Jolly, my dear? We'll go to d'Viff Vlieghen.'

With that Eunice had to be content.

He got up. 'There are a couple of phone calls I must make. Ask Jolly to come to the study, will you, Charity?'

He wandered off and presently Jolly knocked on the study door.

Tyco looked up from his desk. 'Ah, yes, Jolly. We have a little problem.'

He explained about the mythical visitors and added, 'Be sure and tell Mrs Jolly and Nel; we mustn't let *mevrouw* down.'

'Leave it to me, Professor,' said Jolly, and made his stately way to the kitchen where he laid down the law, exclaiming that he for one would be glad to see the back of the young lady. 'Making eyes at the professor,' he said darkly, 'and *mevrouw* such a sweet lady too.'

It wasn't until Tyco had gone to fetch the children that Charity was struck by the thought that if Eunice should mention the expected visitors they might give the game away. She sat with her ears stretched to hear the return of the car and hurried into the hall as they all came in.

Tyco took a look at her worried face. 'Don't panic,' he said placidly. 'They know, and Jolly has dealt with the staff.'

Charity let out a great breath. 'Oh, thank you—it was silly of me.'

He flung a comforting arm around her. 'Don't worry, and the children are delighted.' He kissed her slowly. 'You really are a most resourceful girl.'

That night, as she got ready for bed, Charity reflected upon the day. It had gone well, she considered; Tyco had been at his most amiable, the perfect host, and the children had been angels. She had had difficulty in not giggling when Mrs Jolly had come to ask her if she should see about getting the bedrooms ready for the influx of guests. 'Perhaps we should meet after breakfast tomorrow and approve the menus, *mevrouw*.' She had agreed gravely, conscious of Tyco's eyes on her. She wondered uneasily if she should have invited Eunice to stay for as long as she wished and dismissed the thought; she was already making a play for Tyco and she was very lovely too in an amusing and outrageous fashion.

The evening had been a success though. D'Viff Vlieghen was an ancient warren of rooms housed in five typical Dutch houses. The food had been good and it was packed with diners, most of them foreign and for the most part noisy. She suspected that Tyco would have preferred somewhere quieter but it pleased their guest and that was more important, she supposed. Eunice had bubbled over with delight, aware of the admiring glances in her direction. She had looked quite beautiful in a vivid green dress, her hair brushed into a golden cloud. Charity had known better than to try and compete; she had worn the grey dress, comforted by Tyco's, 'You look very nice, my dear.'

She got up the next morning with a shamefaced relief that in one more day Eunice would be gone. They would go shopping in the morning, she decided, and probably Tyco would take them out in the evening. Light of heart, she skipped along to the children's room.

Teile was dressed but Letizia was curled up in bed with a flushed face and heavy eyes. Charity sat down on her bed and took the little hand in hers. 'Darling, what's up? You should have called me...'

'She's got a sore throat,' said Teile. 'We didn't want to disturb you.'

'I'll fetch your papa. You stay here, love, and if you're dressed and ready, Teile, go down to breakfast, will you? I'll be down presently. I expect it's just a cold.'

Tyco, when he had examined his small daughter, agreed. 'A day in bed, I think, don't you, Charity? I will leave a little later and take Teile to school and Nel can fetch her at noon.'

Which left a grumpy Eunice to take herself off to the shops. She came back for lunch with several dress boxes and made no bones about her disappointment that Tyco wasn't home to admire the contents. She spent the afternoon by the drawing-room fire and was in the hall to greet Tyco when he got home after tea.

He bade her a cheerful hello and went straight upstairs to the children's room where Charity was perched beside Letizia, drawing plans for another dolls' house. Teile was in the schoolroom doing her homework and they were calling to and fro through the open doors. He looked at Charity as he went in; she was untidy, she had kicked off her shoes and her small nose shone, and he smiled a little at the sight of her, his eyes gleaming beneath their lids. As she looked up all he said was, 'Hello. I sneaked home early; how has the day been?'

Letizia had her voice back. 'I'm almost well. Charity says I'll be quite well in two more days. Can Teile come and see me?'

'As long as she doesn't get too close, *liefje*. What are you making?'

He sat down on the bed and examined the house, in no hurry to go, and Charity, conscious of her untidy appearance, said, 'Well, if you're going to be here for a few minutes I'll go and tidy myself.'

'I quite like you as you are,' said Tyco, 'but don't be long, we shall miss you.'

When she got back Tyco said, 'Eunice wants to go to a night-club—shall you like that?'

'I don't know, I've never been to one——'

Letizia's hand shot out and grabbed her arm. 'Don't go out, Charity, please—stay with me. I feel better when you're here.'

'Then I'll stay.' She spoke promptly before Tyco could say anything.

'Papa can take Eunice out—it's her last evening you see and so she must have a treat.'

'You don't mind?' enquired Tyco mildly.

'Mind? Of course not.' She spoke so heartily that it didn't sound true, which it wasn't anyway; she minded very much but he must never guess that she was seething with jealousy and hopeless love.

He eyed her narrowly, 'Good—then I'll take her to the Carousel—we'd better eat out too. Oh, de Silveren Speigel might suit her taste. Plenty of smart people go there; she'll be able to show off her pretty clothes.'

'She'll love that,' said Charity through clenched teeth. 'Do go and tell her while I get this poppet comfortable and make sure Teile has done her homework.'

'Quite the little mother,' sighed Tyco softly.

'Isn't that what you wanted?'

The children in bed, she took time to change her dress and went downstairs in time to see Tyco helping Eunice into a velvet cape. She looked ravishing; there was a glint of scarlet from beneath its folds and she was wearing scarlet slippers. It was Tyco she looked at, though; immaculate in a dinner-jacket, laughing at something Eunice had said. He looked up and saw her and said, 'We're just off, my dear. Don't wait up, you've had a trying day.'

She smiled sweetly and agreed silently. 'Have a lovely time, both of you.' Her voice was as sweet as her smile.

She ate her solitary dinner and read for an hour or so before she went upstairs to her room. A long bath took up another hour but it was still barely eleven o'clock. The children were asleep and she could hear Jolly going around locking up. Presently the house was quiet. She put on her dressing-gown and pattered soundlessly downstairs to make a pot of tea and sit at the kitchen table drinking it. She couldn't spend the night there, so she went back to her room and roamed around, picking up ornaments and putting them down again. The little carriage clock on the mantelshelf had struck one o'clock before she heard the whisper of the car and a moment later the gentle sound of the great front door being closed. Curiosity got the better of good sense; she opened the door a crack. They were still in the hall; she could hear the murmur of their voices and presently Eunice's giggle and then her voice, quite light and clear. 'Darling, it was heaven—has Charity any idea of what fun you are on an evening out? We must do this again some time. Now shall we say goodnight properly?'

Charity was shaking with rage, so that shutting the door was difficult, but she managed it and stood leaning against it. She had never felt so awful in all her life, and the pity of it was that there was no need for her unhappiness; Eunice had seen the thread of light from her room on the gallery wall and had raised her voice deliberately, talking to Tyco's broad back while he read the messages on the hall table, taking no notice of her at all.

CHAPTER NINE

TYCO wasn't at breakfast; Charity was glad that she didn't have to face him. He had been called away early, Jolly told her—four o'clock in the morning. 'And him with barely three hours' sleep,' said his faithful servant.

Charity took Teile to school, leaving Letizia in Nel's kindly hands, and when she got back it was just in time to see Eunice coming, yawning, down the stairs.

'Oh, lord, I could sleep for a week. I got Mrs Jolly to bring me some breakfast in bed—old crosspatch she is too, even though I couldn't understand half she said.'

'Mrs Jolly is our housekeeper, and she has a lot to do for the weekend. She doesn't expect to wait on our guests.'

'Oh, dear, we are high and mighty, aren't we? Well, don't let being Mevrouw van der Brons go to your head. You're nothing but a glorified governess and housekeeper yourself. Tyco must find that you're a dead bore. And the way you suck up to the children...' She gave a snigger. 'Tyco is going over to England, did you know? I thought not. He'll come and see me—I've been lent a friend's flat. We'll go out on the town while you're queening it here with those brats and the housekeeping.' She danced a few steps. 'I told you I'd annex him, didn't I?'

172

Charity went past her and tugged the old-fashioned bell pull in the drawing-room, and when Jolly came she asked, 'At what time did the professor arrange for you to drive Miss Pearson to Schiphol?'

'Her flight leaves at half-past one, *mevrouw*; we ought to leave here soon after noon.'

'Miss Pearson will be leaving as soon as her luggage can be brought down,' said Charity. 'About half an hour—if you would have the car ready by then, please, Jolly.'

'Certainly, *mevrouw*.' Jolly went back to the kitchen to regale his wife with the latest developments. 'I said that young woman would be a mischief-maker—you mark my words, there'll be ructions...'

Eunice said sulkily. 'I've not packed——'

'Then you had better go and do it now.'

Eunice started back up the stairs. 'You're green with envy,' she said, 'not that it matters. I know just how to handle Tyco—all men are alike, only you wouldn't know that, would you? I'll bet a year's fees that he leaves you inside a year—with the kids of course, knowing that they'll be looked after by you while he enjoys life. You told me he loves his work, but he can be a successful surgeon anywhere in the world.' She tossed her head. 'To have tied himself down to you must be one of the few mistakes he has made. Ah, well, you will have had a couple of months with your head in the clouds.'

Charity was standing very still; she might indeed have been carved in stone. Now she said briskly, 'Do go and pack, Eunice,' and then turned on her heel and went into the drawing-room where she stayed until her stepsister came down again.

Eunice said, 'Well, I'm ready to go—a pity about Tyco's family, we were just getting to know each other really well. Still, we can go on from where we left off when he comes to London. I've a boring job there—photos—and then I shall be at a loose end.'

Charity put down the knitting she had been mangling. 'Not for long, I feel sure. You've never liked me and always despised me, haven't you, Eunice? I would be lying if I said that I was sorry to see you go; all the same I hope you have a good flight back. Goodbye.'

Jolly was holding the door open. 'What's the betting he's at the airport to see me off with a bunch of red roses?' she asked as she went through the door.

Charity summoned up a mocking little laugh. All the same, when the car had gone she went back into the small sitting-room, picked up the phone and asked if Professor van der Brons was in the clinic.

He was and she sighed with relief, only to remember then that Eunice's plane didn't go until half-past one and it was only a little after ten o'clock. He would have all the time in the world if he left the hospital at twelve-thirty.

She went upstairs to sit with Letizia and the minutes dragged themselves round to an hour—two hours...at half-past twelve she would ring the hospital again. She hated herself for doing it, going behind his back, spying on him, suspecting him of she knew not what, but she would have no rest until she knew.

At a little after noon Tyco came home. Charity heard his key in the lock and went down to the hall to meet him. 'If you've come to take Eunice to the airport, she's already gone. She left just after ten o'clock; I told her to go and if you're annoyed about that it's just too bad. If you're quick you'll have half an hour with her before she goes on board.'

Tyco was standing quite still, his eyes bright in his placid face. 'Well, well, what have I here? A termagant—and I wonder why?'

'I am not a terma—whatever that is.' Strive as she might to keep her voice steady and quiet, it had become shrill. All her bottled-up feelings came pouring out, despite the fact that she had vowed not to say a word; indeed, she had thought up any number of innocent reasons why Eunice had left early. 'Coming home at one o'clock in the morning——'

'You were awake?'

'Of course I was awake. And I heard Eunice, saying—saying all those things about me, and don't look like that, I had the door open,' she said furiously, 'and if you just wanted a governess for the children why didn't you get one? There was no need to marry me; now you're tied, tied to me, and you're such a successful surgeon you could go wherever you liked in the world and if you made a mistake marrying me then it's your own silly fault.' She drew a heaving breath. 'And what am I going to do if you leave me with the children and how could you ever think of leaving them—leaving me is another matter—but to leave them...?'

'Dear, oh, dear, could we go somewhere and get to the bottom of this?'

She gave a sniff. 'No.' She glanced at him and saw the little smile and the brightness of his eyes. 'And don't you dare laugh...'

'You are so cross I think that we had better leave things as they are for the moment, don't you? Perhaps this evening when you're feeling better we can talk?'

'I don't need to feel better, I feel fine.'

'You are cross—very cross.' He bent suddenly and kissed her gently but she stepped away from him.

'Don't do that,' she said, adding with perfect truth, 'I can't bear it.'

'I must bear that in mind.' He sounded coldly polite. 'I'm going to see Letizia.'

He went past her and up the staircase and left her standing in the hall, appalled at all the things she had said, most of which she hadn't meant.

He would never love her now; she had behaved like a fishwife and she had no right to do so. If she had been his wife—his real wife—then there might have been some excuse, but they had never been any more than good friends and he had never pretended otherwise or given her the idea that he wasn't quite content the way they were.

She went into the dining-room and sat down at the table; Jolly would be bringing their lunch at any moment now.

Jolly was in the kitchen, recounting the scene in the hall. 'For I was passing through the back hall and the baize door was a little open,' he explained to Mrs Jolly and Nel, 'and there she was, bless her, hauling him over the coals and him not knowing why. All on account of that Miss Pearson saying nasty things before she went.' He was speaking in Dutch and his wife answered him in the same language.

'It will clear the air,' she said comfortably. 'Made for each other, they are.'

Teile came dancing in from school presently. When Tyco joined them a little later his manner was exactly as usual and the meal passed off in what appeared to be a most convivial atmosphere. Tyco took Teile back to school as he went, bidding Charity a pleasant goodbye as he left the house.

She would have liked to have gone somewhere quiet and had a good cry but Letizia demanded her company. Charity brought her down for tea in the drawing-room and when Teile came back with Nel the three of them sat around the fire, eating peanut butter sandwiches and Mrs Jolly's chocolate sponge cake.

When Tyco got home the awkwardness Charity felt was lost in the children's chatter and the business of getting them to their beds.

However, that couldn't last forever; she had to go down to the drawing-room at last, to find Tyco, pleasantly casual, waiting with their drinks.

She hadn't known what she had expected but certainly not this placid small talk over dinner, a steady flow of conversation and never a word about Eunice. Their quarrel was to be forgotten, she supposed.

She supposed wrong. She sat down by the small rent table and lifted the coffee-pot and Tyco asked mildly, 'Shall we have our talk?'

She put down the coffee-pot and eyed him stonily. There wasn't much use in pretending that she didn't know what he was talking about. Instead of making some suitable and calm reply she burst out, 'When are you going to London?'

He had gone to lean against the massive carved chimney piece.

'Did Eunice tell you that as well?' He was sounding mildly interested.

She nodded, and he studied the nails of one hand, not looking at her. 'And you believed her?'

She muttered, 'I didn't want to...'

'Why not?'

'Well—I didn't think you'd do something like that, not without telling me. You're not like Cor...'

'I am very relieved to hear that. Did Eunice tell you what we were going to do in London?'

'Oh, yes.' She heaved a great seething sigh. 'You are going out on the town...'

'You believed that too, even although you didn't want to?'

'Yes. I think I did, but I don't blame you; it's such a pity you didn't meet her before me, if you see what I mean...'

'No. I don't see what you mean, all I see is that you no longer trust me.' His voice became icy and she suddenly saw that he was in a towering rage, all the more alarming since it was being held in check by an iron hand. 'I had thought...but no matter.'

Her own temper had died beneath his cool politeness. She said urgently, 'Tyco, do listen. I knew when I married you that I wasn't the kind of wife you needed. I'm plain, you're blind if you can't see that, and I'm not clever or witty, or—or fashionable—no one would turn round and look at me if we went into a restaurant—it must be nice for a man to have a wife whose friends are envious of him. Someone who can dance all night and make you laugh.' Her voice petered out because he was laughing. Real laughter too, a great bellow of mirth.

'My dear girl, will you listen to me?'

'No. Please, Tyco, I don't want to talk any more. I'm sorry I listened to Eunice, I suppose it serves me right that I heard what she said—listeners never hear any good of themselves, do they?' She lifted the coffee-pot and put it down again. 'The coffee's cold. I'm sorry, I'll get Jolly to bring some fresh.'

'Not on my account, Charity. I have some work to do still; I'll say goodnight.'

He had gone before she could utter a word and she sat there, her hands in her lap, looking into the fire and wondering what to do next. She couldn't go away, not yet, because of the children; she didn't want to hurt them, and they were so happy. Besides, she loved him—to go away and never see him again was past bearing. Better to stay; at least she would see him each day. She would apologise when he was no longer angry and do her best to be the kind of wife he wanted. Having made this decision she took herself off to bed and cried herself to sleep.

Letizia was well enough to get up in the morning although it was decided to keep her at home for just one more day. The weather was bad; a raw wind and an icy rain falling from a grey sky.

'I'll take Teile with me,' said Tyco at breakfast. 'I shan't be home for lunch but if the weather is still as bad as it is now Jolly can take the Rover and fetch her at noon. I leave that for you to decide, Charity.'

'Yes, Tyco.' She tried to speak cheerfully. 'Perhaps it will clear later.'

'Possibly. Now, Teile, I am leaving in five minutes...' That was a signal for the child and Charity to get up from the table to fetch coat, hat and school books, and to find gloves. In the flurry of leaving the house, no one noticed that Tyco didn't bid Charity goodbye, only gave her a brief unsmiling nod with the remark that he hoped to be home around five o'clock.

It was unfortunate that Eunice telephoned that morning. Letizia was in the kitchen helping Mrs Jolly to make fairy cakes for tea and Charity was worrying her way through the household books, a task Mrs Jolly seemed to think she should deal with even though the accounts and bills were in Dutch and she needed to use a dictionary more often than not. She picked up the receiver, head full of Dutch groceries.

'Mevrouw van der Brons...'

Eunice sniggered. 'Still there, are you? Have you said anything to Tyco? I bet you haven't had the pluck to ask him if he gave me red roses. I'm going to ring the hospital now and have a little chat with him. Have you got rid of the family yet?' And when Charity didn't answer, she asked, 'Has the cat got your tongue?' Charity put down the phone.

Tyco came home at five o'clock, to all intents and purposes his usual calm self. He didn't kiss her, but then she had already told him in no uncertain terms not to do so, hadn't she? The evening passed as usual: spending the time with the children, seeing them to their beds and then dining together, carrying on a conversation about nothing at all while she did her best to eat the delicious food Mrs Jolly had prepared. It was rather like acting in a play, she reflected when Tyco said pleasantly that he had work to do and took himself off to his study, leaving her to knit the last of the ducks. She had to unpick it the next day, for she hadn't been concentrating, only rehearsing a variety of apologies, none of which sounded quite right.

Several days went by and Charity sought in vain for a chance to speak to Tyco, but his pleasant coolness held her at arm's length and somehow she was unable to find the right moment. Life went on much as usual; they dined out with friends, she held long telephone conversations with various members of his family, saw to the house, painstakingly conned housekeeping bills and discussed, in her halting Dutch, each day's food.

The weather had improved and the children grumbled a good deal because, despite the cold, the ice wasn't safe for skating. Charity took them for brisk walks instead when they were free from school, gaping happily with them at the massive street organ in the Dam Square, spending their half-holidays at the zoo and the aquarium. Her days were filled even if they weren't happy, but they couldn't go on like this, she thought sadly; something would have to be done.

The children had had half-term and she accepted an invitation to have coffee with the *directrice*. Charity, who hadn't forgotten what it was like to be a nurse, was a little in awe, for she met the lady several times but she discovered that being Mevrouw van der Brons was quite a different thing from Zuster Pearson. It seemed strange to sit in the *directrice*'s sitting-room, exchanging small talk while they drank their coffee. She spent a pleasant hour there and then, mindful of fetching the children from school, bade her hostess goodbye and began on the lengthy walk through the hospital to the entrance.

She was very nearly there when Cor van Kamp came out of one of the doors lining the corridor. He stopped in front of her, preventing her from passing him.

'Well, well, Mevrouw van der Brons. I must say you look very smart, not quite up to the standard of an eminent surgeon's wife, but passable—quite passable. Been keeping an eye on him?'

She had nothing to say to that, pausing only long enough to look him in the eye with contempt before walking on.

Tyco, turning on to the far end of the corridor, was in time to see the pair of them standing together. He barely paused in what he was saying to Wim who was with him. 'I think that is all,' he concluded with his usual calm. 'I shall be at home, if I'm wanted. *Dag*, Wim.'

Wim, who had intended going to his car with him, and had seen Charity too, said, '*Dag*, Prof,' and hurried away.

Charity had also seen Tyco; she hurried towards him—there was no one about, perhaps now would be the time...

'What was young van Kamp doing?' demanded Tyco coldly. 'Surely there are more suitable places in which to meet?'

'Meet, him and me? You're joking...' She paused to look at him and saw that he wasn't. 'I've been having coffee with the *directrice*. I was on my way home and Cor came out of a door.' She was suddenly indignant. 'I didn't even speak to him.'

She studied his face: a polite mask, giving nothing away. 'Did you really think that I'd talk to him? Meet him on the sly? Well, I wouldn't, which is more than

I can say for you with your red roses and telephone calls.'

Astonishment swept over Tyco's handsome features.

'Red roses, telephone calls? What do you mean? What are you talking about?'

'At Schiphol, of course; you gave her red roses, she said so, and she telephoned a few days ago and said she was going to phone you at the hospital and you never said a word when you came home.' Her voice had risen; she had a fine colour, and if there had been something handy she would have thrown it at him. So clever and so unable to see the nose on his face. Now the tiresome man was smiling. She stamped a well-shod foot and said, 'Oh, pooh!' and, quite light-headed with misery and the hopelessness of the whole situation, stood on tiptoe and kissed his chin. She couldn't reach higher.

She was almost at the entrance door when he caught up with her, took her by the arm, said something to the porter on duty and bustled her out to the car, shoved her into it, got in beside her and drove off, all without a word.

At the house he chivvied her gently indoors and, when Jolly came into the hall, said, 'Ask Nel to fetch the children, will you, Jolly? And we don't want to be disturbed.'

He took off her gloves, her coat and hat, tossed them on to a chair and said mildly, 'The drawing-room?' He glanced at his watch. 'We have more than half an hour—plenty of time...'

'What for?' asked Charity, who, until that moment, had been unable to think of anything to say. 'Why do we want plenty of time?'

She was standing in the middle of the room and Samson had pranced to meet them. She bent to pat his head because she didn't want to look at Tyco. She must have have been mad to kiss him, whatever must he be thinking.

'Very little time is needed in which to say I love you,' said Tyco, 'but I dare say we can enlarge upon that to our mutual satisfaction.'

He had been standing by the door; now he crossed the room and stood within inches of her. 'My dearest darling, you kissed me.'

She said in a whisper, 'I didn't mean to—it, it just popped out before I could stop it.' She peeped at him and found him smiling. 'You said, "Dearest, darling".'

'So I did, my dearest darling, because that is what you have become. And I suppose you have always been that, only I didn't know it. I am not sure when I knew that, I only know that life without you is unthinkable.'

'You could have said——'

'My love, my very dear love, I am almost seventeen years older than you and there was young van Kamp.'

'Oh, pooh,' said Charity strongly, 'being in love isn't at all the same as infatuation. When you're infatuated you bother about being smartly dressed and amusing and your hair being just so, but being in love is quite different. It doesn't matter because it's you, not clothes or how you look or even if you've got a cold in the head.' She added wildly, 'Oh, do you see what I mean, Tyco?'

'You have put it most plainly, my love.'

'Yes, well. What about Mevrouw de Groot and Eunice . . . ?'

'Let me put your mind at rest. I have never given either of them red roses. I—er—dangled them before you in the hope of arousing your interest in me as a man—as your husband.'

'I've always been interested in you,' she added recklessly, 'and I've been in love with you for weeks and even if you were ninety and on crutches it wouldn't make any difference. But I'm glad you're only forty.'

He wrapped his great arms around her and drew her close. 'I'm glad too.'

He bent to kiss her and kiss her again and she stood within his arms, so suddenly happy that she thought she would never believe it.

The door was opened cautiously and Teile's head poked round it.

'Jolly said not to come in, but we knew you'd want us.'

She opened the door a little wider and Letizia came in too and the pair of them stood surveying them thoughtfully. 'We wanted to ask you something. We'd very much like a baby brother . . .' She smiled widely. 'If you wouldn't mind?'

Charity felt Tyco's arms tighten around her ribs—they would break at any moment, but she didn't care. She looked up at him and met his gaze steadily.

'I don't think we would mind, would we, my darling?' He was smiling down at her and the smile was very tender but there was a gleam in his eyes.

'Not in the least; it would be the final touch to—to...'

'Wedded bliss?' he asked softly.

'Yes,' said Charity.

HARLEQUIN
Romance®

and WEDDINGS go together—
especially in June!
So don't miss next month's title in

THE BRIDAL COLLECTION

LOVE YOUR ENEMY
by Ellen James

THE BRIDE led the anti-Jarrett forces.
THE GROOM was Jarrett!
THE WEDDING? An Attraction of Opposites!

Available this month in
THE BRIDAL COLLECTION

THE MAN YOU'LL MARRY
by Debbie Macomber
Harlequin Romance (#3196)
Wherever Harlequin books are sold.

WED-2

Janet Dailey
Americana

Janet Dailey's perennially popular Americana series continues with more exciting states!

Don't miss this romantic tour of America through fifty favorite Harlequin Presents novels, each one set in a different state, and researched by Janet and her husband, Bill.

A journey of a lifetime in one cherished collection.

June titles   **#33 NORTH CAROLINA**
That Carolina Summer

#34 NORTH DAKOTA
Lord of High Lonesome

If you missed your state or would like to order any other states that have already been published, send your name, address, zip or postal code, along with a check or money order for $3.99 plus 75¢ postage and handling ($1.00 in Canada) for each book ordered, payable to Harlequin Reader Service to:

In the U.S.

3010 Walden Avenue
P.O. Box 1325
Buffalo, NY 14269-1325

In Canada

P.O. Box 609
Fort Erie, Ontario
L2A 5X3

Please specify book title(s) with your order.
Canadian residents add applicable federal and provincial taxes.

JD-JUNE

HARLEQUIN
Romance

Coming Next Month

OVER THE YEARS, TELEVISION HAS BROUGHT
THE LIVES AND LOVES OF MANY CHARACTERS INTO
YOUR HOMES. NOW HARLEQUIN INTRODUCES YOU
TO THE TOWN AND PEOPLE OF

One small town—twelve terrific love stories.

GREAT READING...GREAT SAVINGS...AND A FABULOUS
FREE GIFT!

Each book set in Tyler is a self-contained love story; together, the
twelve novels stitch the fabric of the community.

By collecting proofs-of-purchase found in each Tyler book, you can
receive a fabulous gift, ABSOLUTELY FREE! And use our special
Tyler coupons to save on your next TYLER book purchase.

Join us for the fourth TYLER book,
MONKEY WRENCH by Nancy Martin.

*Can elderly Rose Atkins successfully bring a new love into
granddaughter Susannah's life?*

BIG SUMMER READ

Summer Reading At Its Best

In July, Harlequin and Silhouette bring readers the Big Summer Read Program. Heat up your summer with these four exciting new novels by top Harlequin and Silhouette authors.

SOMEWHERE IN TIME by Barbara Bretton
YESTERDAY COMES TOMORROW by Rebecca Flanders
A DAY IN APRIL by Mary Lynn Baxter
LOVE CHILD by Patricia Coughlin

From time travel to fame and fortune, this program offers something for everyone.

Available at your favorite retail outlet.

BSR

is

 exotic

✓ dramatic

✓ sensual

✓ exciting

✓ contemporary

✓ a fast, involving read

✓ terrific!!

*Harlequin Presents—
passionate romances
around the world!*

"GET AWAY FROM IT ALL" SWEEPSTAKES

HERE'S HOW THE SWEEPSTAKES WORKS

NO PURCHASE NECESSARY

To enter each drawing, complete the appropriate Official Entry Form or a 3" by 5" index card by hand-printing your name, address and phone number and the trip destination that the entry is being submitted for (i.e., Caneel Bay, Canyon Ranch or London and the English Countryside) and mailing it to: Get Away From It All Sweepstakes, P.O. Box 1397, Buffalo, New York 14269-1397.

No responsibility is assumed for lost, late or misdirected mail. Entries must be sent separately with first class postage affixed, and be received by: 4/15/92 for the Caneel Bay Vacation Drawing, 5/15/92 for the Canyon Ranch Vacation Drawing and 6/15/92 for the London and the English Countryside Vacation Drawing. Sweepstakes is open to residents of the U.S. (except Puerto Rico) and Canada, 21 years of age or older as of 5/31/92.

For complete rules send a self-addressed, stamped (WA residents need not affix return postage) envelope to: Get Away From It All Sweepstakes, P.O. Box 4892, Blair, NE 68009.

© 1992 HARLEQUIN ENTERPRISES LTD.   SWP-RLS

"GET AWAY FROM IT ALL" SWEEPSTAKES

HERE'S HOW THE SWEEPSTAKES WORKS

NO PURCHASE NECESSARY

To enter each drawing, complete the appropriate Official Entry Form or a 3" by 5" index card by hand-printing your name, address and phone number and the trip destination that the entry is being submitted for (i.e., Caneel Bay, Canyon Ranch or London and the English Countryside) and mailing it to: Get Away From It All Sweepstakes, P.O. Box 1397, Buffalo, New York 14269-1397.

No responsibility is assumed for lost, late or misdirected mail. Entries must be sent separately with first class postage affixed, and be received by: 4/15/92 for the Caneel Bay Vacation Drawing, 5/15/92 for the Canyon Ranch Vacation Drawing and 6/15/92 for the London and the English Countryside Vacation Drawing. Sweepstakes is open to residents of the U.S. (except Puerto Rico) and Canada, 21 years of age or older as of 5/31/92.

For complete rules send a self-addressed, stamped (WA residents need not affix return postage) envelope to: Get Away From It All Sweepstakes, P.O. Box 4892, Blair, NE 68009.

© 1992 HARLEQUIN ENTERPRISES LTD.   SWP-RLS

"GET AWAY FROM IT ALL"

Brand-new Subscribers-Only Sweepstakes

OFFICIAL ENTRY FORM

This entry must be received by: April 15, 1992
This month's winner will be notified by: April 30, 1992
Trip must be taken between: May 31, 1992—May 31, 1993

YES, I want to win the Caneel Bay Plantation vacation for two. I understand the prize includes round-trip airfare and the two additional prizes revealed in the BONUS PRIZES insert.

Name _____

Address _____

City _____

State/Prov. _____ Zip/Postal Code _____

Daytime phone number _____
(Area Code)

Return entries with invoice in envelope provided. Each book in this shipment has two entry coupons — and the more coupons you enter, the better your chances of winning!

© 1992 HARLEQUIN ENTERPRISES LTD.   1M-CPN